I0663042

Field Work

Books by John D. Nesbitt

For the Norden Boys
Lonesome Range
Black Hat Butte
Red Wind Crossing
Rancho Alegre
Raven Springs
Coyote Trail
Black Diamond Rendezvous
Man from Wolf River
Not a Rustler
West of Rock River
North of Cheyenne
Poacher's Moon
Adventures of the Ramrod Rider
A Good Man to Have in Camp
Keep the Wind in Your Face
Shadows on the Plain
Field Work
Blue Horse Mesa: Western Stories
Antelope Sky: Stories of the Modern West
Seasons in the Fields: Stories of a Golden West

Two Novellas:
"Dead for the Last Time"
"Trouble in the Labor Camp"

Field Work

John D. Nesbitt

SPEAKING VOLUMES, LLC
NAPLES, FLORIDA
2016

Field Work

Copyright © 2012 by John D. Nesbitt

All rights reserved. No part of this book may be reproduced or transmitted in any form or by any means without written permission of the author.

ISBN 978-1-62815-473-3

for Tommie Fulton,

good friend in those early years

Acknowledgments

"Drifter from Wenatchee" appeared in *Beat to a Pulp: Round Two* (2012).

"Paddle Your Own Canoe" appeared in *Roundup!* (Cheyenne: La Frontera Publishing, 2010).

"Killing for Chocolate" appeared in *Hardboiled*, #44 (February 2012).

"At the End of the Orchard" appeared in *Hardboiled*, #40 (May 2009).

"Boom-Boom" appeared in *Mysterical-E* online magazine (Summer 2011).

Table of Contents

Drifter from Wenatchee

I was sitting on the steps outside my room when a stranger pulled into the auto court in a yellow-and-white Chrysler. He parked in front of number 23, which had been vacant, and went inside with a brown bag of groceries. A little while later, Roxanne came out and sat in a metal chair in front of room 21. She did that just about every night while her father and mother and brother sat inside drinking beer and watching a black-and-white television. I went over to talk to her, hoping as usual that I would get next to her one of these nights.

Roxanne was a dishwater blonde with a pale complexion for someone who worked in the fields. This evening she was wearing a sleeveless white blouse and sand-colored shorts, so her pale legs were noticeable.

"Hi," I said. "How'd it go today?"

"About the same. And you?"

I shrugged. "About normal." She and her family were picking peaches just as I was, but for a different outfit, and it was rare that anything new happened either in the orchard or in the camp.

"It got hot today."

"Oh, yeah," I said. "I drank a lot of water."

She lit a cigarette, and her mouth held the shape of an "O" as she blew the smoke away. Then her eyes looked past me.

I turned to see a guy with dark hair slicked back on the sides and over on top. He was wearing a gold-colored shirt with the collar turned up and the short sleeves cuffed. As he strolled toward Roxanne, I noticed the name "Carol" above his left bicep.

He was an older guy in his mid-thirties, and he had a cock-sure air about him. He ignored me as he lifted his head and tossed a glance at Roxanne. "Hey, there," he said. "My name's Vince. I just moved in next door." He pointed with his thumb at number 23.

She said, "Uh-huh," but she didn't look at him.

His head swayed. "Just thought I'd say hello."

She looked up at him with her mouth twisted and her eyebrows drawn, but she didn't say anything.

His voice had a down-home accent when he said, "You look kinda cute when you give me that go-to-hell look."

I didn't care for his kind of hustle, so I said, "I bet you get a lot of 'em."

His face went hard, and he gave me a cold stare. "I don't get any from the likes of you, buddy."

I shut up. I knew he could kick my ass, and he seemed ready to prove it.

He moved his head back toward her. "What's your name?"

"Roxanne."

"Roxie," he said. "Roxie-Doxie."

She took a puff on her cigarette.

"Well, it's nice to meet you," he said. "I'll come back when you can talk more. Maybe we'll go for a spin. Have a milkshake or somethin'. Don't you think?"

"I don't know."

He strolled away, doing a kind of hoodlum walk I'd seen in the movies.

When he went inside, I said to Roxanne, "That guy thinks he's pretty smart."

"He's just tryin' to be friendly."

"Yeah, I noticed."

* * * * *

The couple on the other side of me in 29 worked in the same orchard I did. The man's name was Jimmy. He was about fifty, a typical guy in field work except that he had a young Mexican wife. He told me he met her through an ad in a magazine. She was somewhere near thirty-five, I'd guess, and her name was Celestina. He called her Sally.

When we took a break at mid-morning, Celestina went to the can. Jimmy sat on the second rung of his ladder, lit a cigarette, and spoke in his squeaky Texan voice.

"You know that feller that moved in last night? Well, he's no stranger, and I'll tell ya, I don't think he's up to any good."

"Do you know him from somewhere else?"

"Wenatchee. He was pickin' cheeries where we were. Had his eye on Sally, I could tell. 'Course, he never got anywhere, but that don't stop his kind."

3

I didn't wonder why he took the trouble to tell me that the guy didn't get anywhere. I hadn't been all that impressed with Celestina's love for her husband. She was gloomy most of the time and spoke to him in a cross voice. If I was older I might have seen more in her, because she had a nice figure. But she didn't seem to care for me, and I didn't worry about her at all. As for Jimmy, he reminded me of the saying that there was no fool like an old fool. I had the basic feeling that she would leave him some day, and it didn't make me feel sorry.

"Do you think he followed you down here?" I asked.

"Could be. I bleeve he knew where we were goin' next."

I didn't doubt that. A lot of people like Jimmy followed a pattern—pick cherries in Stockton, go up to Washington and pick some more, come back down here to work in the peaches or pears, and so on. The government called them migrants, but the common term was fruit tramps.

Jimmy took another drag. He had small, narrow eyes, kind of a washed-out blue, and he squinted as he nodded his head. "I don't think he'll git anywhere, though, not with Sally. If she pisses up the rope on me, she won't get her papers."

* * * * *

Back at the court that evening, I told Roxanne she might want to be careful with this guy Vince. I didn't give her particulars, but I told her Jimmy knew him from before and thought he could be trouble.

"Don't talk too loud," she said. "He's in there drinkin' beer with my dad."

I felt a sinking in my stomach, but I tried not to show it. "He moves pretty fast, huh?"

"He works on the same crew as we do, so he met my dad that way."

"Well, just a word to the wise."

"No need to worry about me."

I hung around for a few minutes more until Vince came out doing his hoodlum walk. He flinched when he saw me, but he raised his head and ignored me as he tapped Roxanne on the arm.

"Hey, babe, your dad says you can go for a spin with me. What do you think?"

"I don't know."

"We won't be gone long. Just get a six-pack." He wagged his eyebrows. "Come on."

"Oh, O.K."

* * * * *

I was sulking in my room a little later on when I heard a knock on the door. When I opened it, Vince was standing on the step.

"Come outside for a minute."

"What for?"

"I've got something to say to you." He stood with his arms bent, like he was ready for action.

"You can say it from where you are."

His hand came from nowhere, and he grabbed me by the front of the shirt. He dragged me out through the doorway, switched hands, and punched me on the left side of my face. I stumbled and fell down.

"That's for sayin' shit about me," he said.

Jimmy's voice came up from behind. "That's enough! Leave that kid alone. Come in here startin' trouble."

Vince turned halfway and sneered at him. "Aw, shut up."

Jimmy had most of his teeth, but his lips pushed together like an old gummer's. His voice was high-pitched and loud. "Shut up your own self. Better yet, git out. No one wants you here."

Vince used both hands to grab Jimmy by the shirt, swing him halfway around, and slam him up against the building. "Don't make me hit you, you old fuck." He let go of Jimmy and walked away.

Jimmy's voice rose again. "You stay away from me, and my wife too. No one needs you."

Vince stopped and turned. His chest was heaving up and down, and I could see it took an effort for him not to do any more. He gave Jimmy a scowl and went into his room.

Jimmy took a couple of steps toward me as he brushed at his shirt. "Just a drifter. That's what he is. And a trouble-maker."

* * * * *

Roxanne was snippy with me when I tried to talk to her the

next evening. "You and Jimmy, one of you's as bad as the other. Stirrin' things up."

The Chrysler was gone, so I said what I thought. "Us? Casanova here, he's the one that caused all the trouble. That's what I get for warnin' you. If you ask me, I think you're a fool to have anything to do with him."

She rolled her eyes. "Well, I'll do what I want, and I don't have to ask you."

I took a close look at her. I felt as if I just then knew something about her. "You're probably fool enough to run off with him."

She wagged her head as she blew out a breath of smoke. "Even if I did, it shouldn't be anything to you."

* * * * *

I didn't talk to her for about three days, and I tried not to pay any attention to what she did. But I saw her coming and going with Vince a couple of times, and I hoped like hell she didn't throw herself away on someone like him.

* * * * *

I was sitting on the steps in front of my room when I heard loud voices in Jimmy's cabin and saw Celestina come out with a pair of suitcases. They were the old pasteboard type, light tan with brown leather corners. She set them down in front of the doorway and went back inside.

I had seen Vince leave on foot about ten minutes earlier, so I didn't know what to make of Celestina packing her bags. For all I knew, it was something she did when she and Jimmy got into an argument. And from the way I'd heard his voice go up and stay on a whiny pitch, I thought he might have been drinking.

The next time Celestina came out, she had two grocery sacks crammed full. She set them next to the suitcases and stood there.

Jimmy came to the doorway and said, "Put that stuff back inside. You're not goin' anywhere."

"I do what I want," she said.

"Well, so do I." He walked the few steps to his car, unlocked the door, and got in. It was a 1954 Ford, brown and white. He kept it backed into its parking place like some people did, in case the battery went dead and he had to push-start it. So he was on the other side of the car from where I was sitting, and I couldn't see him very well.

A few minutes later, Vince came walking along. He was carrying a paper bag with a carton of cigarettes sticking out. He seemed to change his pace as he turned into the auto court, and he was gazing in the direction of room 21 where Roxanne and her family lived.

Jimmy started up his car, and I didn't think much of it even when I heard him slip it into gear. He rolled out of the parking place, and when he was in the middle of the lot he goosed it. He headed straight at Vince.

I was impressed by how quick Vince was. He didn't turn and stare. He took two quick strides toward the cabins, and when he saw the car still bearing down on him, he jumped into the air. The nose of the Ford hit him on the legs, and he flopped onto the hood. The carton of cigarettes went sailing.

Jimmy slammed on the brakes, and the motor died.

Vince scrambled off the hood, went around to the driver's side, and yanked the door open. Jimmy leaned away and batted at Vince with his hand, but Vince got a hold of him and dragged him out of the car.

Celestina was shouting, "Yeemee, you crazy, you stupid."

People came out of almost every room in the auto court. Someone hollered, "Call the cops," and someone else said, "Let 'em fight."

Vince hit Jimmy three or four times until the old man fell down. Then Vince piled on him and started hitting him with both fists.

Now Celestina was yelling, "Don't hit him. You going to hurt him."

Vince didn't let up, though, and it was sickening the way everyone just stood and watched. I knew I was in for a few punches myself, but I jumped in to try to get Vince off of Jimmy.

It worked better than I thought. As soon as I tackled Vince, he left Jimmy alone and went to work on me. He pushed me off, got to his feet, and came at me swinging. He hit me solid on each side of the face, and I went down.

When I got back on my feet, Jimmy was leaning into his car and reaching under the driver's seat. He came out with a lug wrench.

His voice was high-pitched and shaky as he said, "Now, you son of a bitch, we'll see how tough you are. See what you say to this."

Vince stood there with his eyes narrowed.

"Come on," Jimmy said. "Step up."

"Maybe I will." Vince walked to the passenger's side of his Chrysler, unlocked the door, and opened the glove box. He had a full audience when he turned around and pointed a dark-barreled pistol at Jimmy.

It sure stopped me, and the whole auto court went quiet. I caught a glimpse of Celestina, and she had the kind of expression on her face that you would expect a woman to have when the cops told her they arrested her husband for having a girl buried in the cellar. If she had had even half an idea of taking off with Vince before, it was gone now.

Jimmy's voice came out, squeaky but not as shaky as before. "You're real brave with that thing in your hand."

"Shut up."

"Real brave."

"Don't think I don't know how to use it." Vince looked around at me and Celestina and came back to Jimmy. "It's just not worth it with any of you. But don't push me." He lowered the gun, turned back toward his car, and pushed the door shut. Then he went into his room.

Roxanne's father walked out to the parking lot, picked up the carton of Lucky Strikes, and set it on the hood of the Chrysler. Jimmy started his Ford and backed it into its place while Celestina carried her bags and suitcases inside. Others around the court went into their rooms, and so did I.

I left my door open, though, and about half an hour later I heard Vince come out of his room. From where I sat I could see him as he opened the doors on the driver's side of his car. Within a few minutes he had his stuff packed up and was gone.

* * * * *

Things seemed to get back to normal. Roxanne sat outside the next day, so I went over and talked to her. She said Vince was gone from the picking crew and she guessed he'd moved on.

We chatted for a few minutes more, and when she mentioned that she was out of cigarettes, I offered to drive her to the store. She said that was fine, so I started up my '50 Chevy as she went inside to get some money.

I liked having a girl in my car, and she didn't seem to be in any hurry. I drove the length of town and back, then pulled into the Chinaman's market, where she got out and bought two packs of Marlboros.

When she was back in the car, I asked her if she wanted to drive around some more.

"Might as well," she said. "Nothin' else to do."

I drove out south of town until I came to a turnout. It was shaded by a grove of eucalyptus trees, and it looked like a good spot. I turned in and came to a stop.

We had both windows rolled down. She lit a cigarette and tossed out the match.

"Do you ever think about just goin' someplace?" she said.

"Oh, sure. But it takes money. Where would you go?"

11

"Up to Reno."

"I don't know what kind of work there is up there."

"Jesus," she said. "I'd want to go somewhere where you don't have to work."

"Someone would have to work at some point."

"Oh, I guess."

"I went on a vacation once," I said. "Me and another guy. We worked for a month straight, no days off, and we saved our money. Then we went to the coast. Fort Bragg."

"What was that like?"

"Cool weather. Almost cold, after being here in the valley."

"That's the way Reno and Tahoe are."

To get to Reno and Tahoe, you had to go east up into the Sierras. To get to Fort Bragg, you went west over the Coast Range. I liked the idea of Fort Bragg better. Reno and Tahoe sounded like a lot of money.

"Over on the coast," I said, "you don't have to do anything. Some people fish, or go for abalone. We just loafed around. Watched the waves come in. Built a little fire on the beach."

"That sounds all right. 'Course there's more to do in Reno."

"You could go one place one time, another place the next time."

She nodded and didn't say any more until she finished her cigarette. "Well, I guess I'd better get back, so they don't think I'm doin' anything."

* * * * *

Two nights later in the same spot I got her into the back seat, and things went the way I hoped. She had better movement than some girls I had been with, and I wondered where she learned it. I wasn't sure I wanted to know, though, so I kept my questions to myself and enjoyed what I could.

When we were in the front seat headed back to town, I said, "You ought to think about goin' to the coast. Nothin' to do except lay around the motel room and walk along the beach. Eat some seafood."

"It would be all right."

She didn't sound very eager, and I guess I was jealous for a minute. I said, "Maybe someone else has you talked into going to Reno."

She leaned forward out of the draft to light a cigarette. When she blew away the smoke she said, "I wouldn't go anywhere with someone that had a gun."

I didn't find her very convincing. First, she could have run off with the guy before she knew he had a gun, and second, I thought she was capable of going off with him anyway. He was the type to put stars in her eyes. But I didn't say anything. I thought about that nice magical moment when I got her shorts off, and I hoped I would get to do it again.

* * * * *

I didn't get a chance the next couple of evenings, but every-thing seemed normal until I came home from work the third day. Her family was standing outside and talking to the neigh-bors. As soon as I got out of my car, her father called me over.

He was a light-haired man with a pot belly. His name was Hershel, and he smoked Pall Malls. He had one bobbing in his lips when I walked up to him.

"Have you seen Roxanne?" he asked.

"No, I haven't. Why?"

"She disappeared last night. I didn't know if she went somewhere with you."

I shook my head. "No, not at all. Last time I saw her was yesterday evening. She said she didn't want to go anywhere."

"Well, she must've went somewhere. She wasn't here this morning, and neither was you."

"I went to work. I was gone by about five-thirty."

Hershel looked at his wife and back at me.

I said, "You can ask Jimmy and his wife. They were on the next row."

"We looked for her all day," he said.

"I hope she didn't take off with that drifter."

"Who? Halterman?"

"Vince. I don't know his last name."

"That's him. But I think he's gone."

"I don't know. He could have come back." I thought the action with Roxanne was good enough to make him want to, but I kept that to myself.

I went to my room, got cleaned up, and reheated some spaghetti for dinner. All that time I was thinking about Roxanne and how I hoped she had more sense than go somewhere with that guy.

* * * * *

I woke up in the middle of the night. Something was strange. The swamp cooler was rumbling like always, but a cool, hard object was pressed against my face between my cheekbone and my nose. Someone else was in the room, next to my bed.

A small flashlight came on. I saw that the object was a gun, and the person holding it was Vince.

"What do you want?" I asked.

"Get up."

"What for?"

"Because I said so." He stood back and kept the gun leveled at me.

I sat up and swung my legs around.

"Get dressed."

My head was clearing. I wondered how he got into my room, and I figured a guy like him could pick the lock on any door in the court. "What's goin' on?" I asked.

"I said get dressed."

"Why?"

"I already told you why."

I put on the clothes I had laid out before I went to sleep. When I finished tying my shoes, he spoke again.

"Get your car keys. And don't do anything stupid, or you'll get this thing in the guts." He motioned with the gun.

When we stepped outside, he said, "You're drivin'. Open my door first, then go around and open yours. You get in, and then I will."

I did as he said. My interior light didn't work, but I found the ignition next to the steering column, poked the key in, and turned it on. I stepped on the clutch and hit the starter button, and the engine fired right up.

"Don't turn on the lights till you're about to pull out onto the road."

I backed the car around, drove to the edge of the lot, and switched on the lights.

"Turn right."

I eased onto the highway. The night was warm and the inside of the car was musty, so I rolled down my window. The town was asleep. I drove south, past the turnout spot, and still didn't see any headlights.

After about three miles he told me to turn left. I drove through farm country, where there were orchards and hay-fields. He had me turn right and left down dirt roads and then right onto a canal road. Out in the middle of nowhere, I saw the reflection of my lights on the bumper and tail lights of a car.

Closer, I saw that it was his Chrysler.

"Pull right up behind it," he said. "Leave the lights on, but shut off the motor and give me the key."

I left the car in gear when I shut if off. When I handed him the key, he told me to stay put. He got out, walked around in front of my car through the headlights, and came to my window.

He pointed the gun at me and said, "Get out." When I did, he herded me into the narrow space between the two cars. "Stop there." He shifted the gun to his left hand and stuck a key into the trunk latch of the Chrysler. He clicked the lock, and the lid lifted.

In the glow of the headlights I saw a body bent and turned away. Without seeing her face, I recognized the light-colored hair and clothes of Roxanne. My stomach was in a knot, and my heart was pounding.

"Lift her out of there."

"What?"

He straight-armed me, hitting me on the side of the head with the heel of his hand. As I gained my balance he said, "Look here, you punk. I'm not fucking around with you. Either you lift her out, or I put a bullet through you."

I reached over and pushed her shoulder, and she was stiff. I braced my legs against the back of the Chrysler as I pulled and shifted and got the dead weight up into my arms.

"Carry her around back of your car."

He followed me, then got ahead and unlocked my trunk.

I lowered her in, and he pushed the lid closed. The hinge made a squeak, and the latch clicked.

"Now get back in the car like before."

As I did that, he walked forward, slammed his trunk closed, and opened his driver's door. He took out a brown paper bag and a red plastic cup that must have come off of a thermos bottle.

He crossed in front of the headlights again and got into my car on the right side. "Shut off the lights," he said.

The night went dark. I heard him crack the seal on the bottle and pour liquid into the cup.

"Drink this."

I took a sip. It was whiskey.

"Drink it. Down the hatch."

I almost choked, but I got it down. I sat for a couple of minutes in the strange silence and breathed with my mouth open. I could feel the alcohol like a cloud in my mouth.

"Give me the cup." He poured more whiskey into it and handed it to me. "Drink it."

"I can't. I just drank a cupful."

"I don't care. Drink some more."

I pulled in some fresh air, then chugged the whiskey. It burned my throat on the way down, and my stomach churned so bad I thought I was going to puke, but I held it down.

"Give it here."

I gave him the cup.

After another long moment, he spoke. "She said you fucked her."

"I don't see where that makes any difference."

"You will." He unscrewed the cap on the bottle. "She said you told her I was no good."

"I don't remember exactly what I said."

"You shit." He poured more whiskey, then sat there in silence as if to say that nothing was going to happen until he said so.

I was getting drunk fast, and I tried to think straight. As I sat in the dark car out on a canal road in the middle of nowhere with a guy sitting next to me holding a gun, the idea that Roxanne was dead seemed all too normal. It made sense that he would have done something like that, but I couldn't form a clear idea of why.

I wondered what his plan was, whether he was trying to make me drink myself to death or whether he wanted to get me falling-down drunk and then shoot me. Either way, I was sure he planned to leave me there dead, with Roxanne in my trunk.

"Here."

"I can't drink any more."

"You just think you can't. I said drink it, or I'll splatter your brains all over the inside of this car."

I took the cup, and the smell almost gagged me. I held the cup near my mouth, but I couldn't make myself drink the whiskey.

He leaned toward me and made like he was going to jab me with the gun. "Quit dickin' around," he said. "Drink it."

I forced the whiskey down, but it came right back up. I got the door open just as I heaved. I coughed and sputtered and vomited some more. My eyes were watery, and I saw little circles in the dark.

"Pick up the cup."

I realized it had hit the ledge of the door and fallen on the ground. I had my right hand on the steering wheel, and my head was leaning out through the open door. "I don't think I can reach it," I said.

19

"Lean down and pick it up. Don't piss me off."

As I reached with my left hand, I lost my grip on the steering wheel. I fell out on the ground.

Vince opened the door on his side, and the next moment he was kicking at me. "Get up, you worthless puke."

"I can't."

He voice was close to me as he said, "The fuck you can't." He poked the barrel of the pistol under my left cheekbone. It pulled me together. Somewhere in the center of my drunk self I found a clear spot. I got up onto my feet, grabbed the steering wheel, and pulled myself into the car. I tried to steady myself as I sat on the corner of the driver's seat.

"Get your feet in."

When I pulled them inside, he slammed the door and went back around the front.

From the clear spot inside me, two things came up that I knew about my car. I could start it in gear with no clutch if the ignition was on, and since I had pulled the key out in the straight-up position, I could turn the switch without the key. As Vince walked between the two cars and set his pistol hand on the hood of my Chevy, I turned on the ignition with my right hand and pushed the starter button with my left.

The car lurched, jammed him into the Chrysler, and lurched again. The gun clunked across the hood and rolled off the right fender.

Vince's scream filled the night. He banged his fist on the hood, then hollered, "Get me out of this."

I realized I had him pinned. I hadn't thought of anything beyond just hitting him with the car. The clear spot in my

20

mind told me I needed to make myself move. I opened the door and got out, and I almost fell over.

He yelled again. "Get me out of here, you fucker, or I'll kill you."

I leaned over, took a full breath of air, and heaved out another gush of whiskey. When Vince pounded on the hood again, I got moving.

I walked for what I thought was a long time, and I still heard him banging. When I got to where the canal road met the dirt road, I didn't hear him anymore.

I followed the dirt roads as well as I could remember, and I came to a paved road where the faintest light was showing in the east. I started walking in the other direction, toward town.

In a little while, a pair of headlights came into view. A car was coming my way. When I waved it down, I saw it was an old pickup. The driver had his window rolled down, and the lights from his dashboard cast a glow on him and the dog in his lap. The man had a clean-shaven farmer's face, and he wore eyeglasses and a canvas cap. The dog was a fluffy grey thing. The music from the radio echoed in the metal cab, and I recognized Dean Martin singing "Everybody loves somebody sometime."

The driver's voice sounded neighborly and calm as he said, "What do you need?"

"A ride to town if I can get it."

"Are you in trouble?"

"Not as much as some people. But I need to talk to some cops."

"Well," he said, "get in. I guess those cows can wait a little while."

Paddle Your Own Canoe

I met this guy named Arlie Buford in the prune orchard. We were working behind the machine, picking into small boxes, so it was something a guy could do by himself. Buford had the row next to mine on the right, and he kept about the same pace as I did. The row on my left had a man and his kid, about sixteen, working together. The two of them got out ahead of us the first morning, so I didn't see much of them. But I saw Buford off and on all day. He didn't have a water jug, but the boss left off a ten-gallon can, the galvanized kind with two handles, and in the afternoon I helped Buford go back and carry it up to where we were working. Then we took a break at the same time.

He drank from a tin can that hung from the handle on a wire hook. I drank from my one-gallon Clorox jug that I filled and put in the freezer compartment every night. I knew what it was like to drink warm water out of a hot can when the temperature was over a hundred, so I offered him a drink out of my jug. He said, no, he was fine. Then he shook out an L&M and lit it. He had his hair combed back on top and on the sides, and he didn't wear a cap or hat. From the looks of him, I thought he'd be just as natural working in a tire shop or pool hall as in a prune orchard.

"This isn't too bad," I said. "But nobody's gonna get rich at it."

He flicked his ashes, and his blue eyes had a faraway shine as he said, "Not you or me, anyway."

I didn't know how to take that, so I said, "Did the boss give you any idea about how long this'll last?"

"Oh, I'd say about two weeks."

He stared off at his row of trees, and I got another look at him. He had light skin that blushed more than it tanned, and his hair was somewhere between blond and light brown. I figured him for a good five years older than I was, which doesn't seem like much, but when you're just nineteen, someone twenty-four or twenty-five might have been around and seen a lot more.

Still, I felt I had more experience in this area than he did. For one thing, I knew to wear a hat. Mine was a regular straw hat, which was fine for working on the ground. If I'd been working on a ladder I'd have worn a cap. This guy didn't wear either one, or even bring his own water, and he didn't seem to know that prune season lasted at least a month. But I figured there were plenty of things he knew that I didn't, so we were probably pretty even where we were.

As we got to talking, I found out this was the first time he had done any kind of orchard work. That didn't matter much, though, because a fella could learn just about any of these jobs in a few minutes, or at least learn what he was supposed to do. After that, it was a matter of getting the hang of it.

Take this work we were doing. The machines went through first—a shaker and a set of catch-frames that got eighty to ninety percent of the fruit. Some years the fruit shook better than others, and a year like this one, guys like us had to strip the trees with long poles. There were a few tricks to that. Then when the tree was stripped, a guy picked up all the scatters—some of them he knocked down himself, and others had fallen past the reach of the catch-frames. After that he picked up the strip of fruit that fell from the gap between the two frames, and the little heap around the trunk, and then there was usually a handful of prunes in the fork of the tree.

All the fruit went into lug boxes, stacked so there was room for the wagon to come through with the swampers. On this job they gave us a piece of chalk to write our number on the end of every box. My number was forty-nine, and I had blue chalk. Buford had yellow-orange chalk, and his number was thirty-seven. At twenty-five cents a box, we were both making about a dollar and a half an hour, which was two bits more than if we were getting paid by the hour.

It didn't take much brains, just the desire to stick with it and try to make a living. None of it ever lasted very long, so a guy made as much as he could. After all, I figured if I was going to get up at five in the morning and put up with the heat and the mosquitoes all day, I might as well make the most of it.

Buford finished his second cigarette, and we both went back to work. We didn't stop or talk for the next couple of hours. When we knocked off at five, he asked me if he could get a ride into town. I said sure. I wondered how he'd gotten out to the orchard that morning, but I didn't ask. As a general rule, I don't ask a lot of questions. I don't want to seem like I'm prying, and most of the time I figure I'll never see this person again anyway, so whatever he tells me on his own is good enough. Then I can decide how much of it to believe.

My old Oldsmobile was hot as an oven inside, so we rolled down the windows and I stepped on the gas. Buford told me he was staying at the Star Hotel, which was an old hotel off Main Street, the kind that charged two or three dollars a night for a small room with the bathroom down the hall. I asked him if he had a way to get to work the next morning, and he said no. I offered to pick him up.

"That'd be damn good," he said. "If you want to get some gas now, I'll chip in."

He gave me a dollar, and I put up two more. Gas was twenty-nine cents a gallon, so my gas gauge was looking better when I pulled out of the station. I left Buford off in front of his hotel, and I drove to my cabin court.

First thing I did was fill my plastic jug and put it in the freezer compartment. Then I opened a can of macaroni and put it on to heat while I fried two slices of Spam. The cabin was hot and stuffy, and it took the squirrel-cage swamp cooler a good ten minutes to put out cool air.

It was all right, though. The place was costing me forty a month for a little kitchen and a main room. I could have had it for fifteen a week, but I went ahead and paid for a month, figuring I'd save money one way or the other. It had an iron-rail bed with bare springs and a mattress, plus a dresser and a narrow couch. The showers and toilets were all together in the middle of the court. It was a place for working men. I never saw anyone who looked like a bum, and I never saw a woman go in or out of any of the rooms.

After I cleaned the dishes I went and took a shower. When I came back, Slim was sitting in front of his cabin. He was an older man about forty-five or fifty, not as tall as most guys who went by Slim, and not all that skinny, just slender. I figured he got the name when he was young, and it stuck. He was an old-time Cat skinner with a weathered face and squinty eyes. He wore khaki shirts and smoked Pall Malls.

"Hello, Tom," he said. "Do any good today?"

"Regular, I guess."

"As much as you can expect. Hotter'n a son of a bitch, ain't it?"

"Sure is." I glanced at the water jug sitting next to his chair with water seeping onto the cement. It was a one-gallon wine jug with a burlap sack sewed tight around. I could see he had filled it and wet down the burlap, and I imagined he would wet it down again before he left in the morning. I knew that kind of jug, how to keep from chipping the mouth of it on a faucet when you filled it, but I knew what it was like when the jug broke, too. Then it was a bundle of crunching glass. Time to get another burlap bag and bum a jug from the sheepherders. Slim was a neat, careful guy, but everyone with a jug like that would break one sooner or later. Drop it on the pavement, crack it on the track of the Caterpillar.

"I'm gonna go in and watch T.V. in a little while," he said. "Come by if you want."

"Thanks, Slim. I don't know if I will tonight."

"Some other time."

"Sure." I went into my cabin and hung my towel to dry. I was wearing a clean shirt and pants, so I got my wallet from my work pants and stepped out into the evening.

Two blocks from the cabin court was a Frostie stand. The girl who worked there didn't look down her nose at me, so I'd gone there a few times. She was by herself again this evening, so I smiled as I stepped up to the window.

"Chocolate?"

"Yep."

I watched her as she swirled the soft ice cream onto the cone. She was just a normal-looking girl in her white uniform, with her blond hair tied back and her face not all done up with make-up. Her blue eyes didn't skate away as she handed me the cone and took the quarter I set on the ledge.

"Here you go."

"Thanks, Patty."

"Thank you. We'll see you later."

She slid the window shut, and I walked back to the cabin court as I ate the ice cream and cone. No hurry, I thought, and even if I did get the nerve to ask her out, there was always the chance she would turn me down.

* * * * *

I heard Slim moving around in the next room before my alarm went off, and I heard him pull out in his old Plymouth while I was making my sandwiches. He was off to a day of sun and dust, diesel fumes, and the ear-splitting crack of a D7 or D8. I had done some of that, and whenever I thought of it I could still hear the noise of the engine, along with the creak and clack of the tracklayer. Slim said none of it bothered him, he just stuffed his ears with cotton and lined up the radiator cap with a mountain peak on the other side of the valley, and pulled the throttle.

Knocking prunes was peaceful work by comparison, with the sound of the machinery at the other end of the orchard like the gunfire in a war movie. It was still lousy work, though. You never knew when you were going to stick your fingers in a prune that had fallen a week earlier. You went right into the mush, and then you were sticky with prune juice, but time was money so you didn't try to keep your hands clean. Even if you did, there would be another rotten prune beneath the ripe ones in the crotch of the tree. So your hands were sticky one way or the other, even when your palms rubbed clean with the knocking pole and the lug boxes, and when you picked the fruit off the ground, the dirt crusted on the sides and backs of your fingers. Then you slapped a mosquito and got a smudge on your face, and so on. It was no place to stay clean or look good. But it didn't matter.

I pulled out of the cabin court at five-thirty. The town was quiet and still like small towns are before sunup. Buford was waiting on the sidewalk with a little bundle of lunch wrapped up in a paper bag. When I stopped, he took a last drag on his cigarette and flipped it away, sending a few sparks along. He got into the passenger's side, and we rolled out of town. Lights had come on in a few houses, but no one was out and about. It gave a fellow a superior feeling, for what little it was worth, to be going to work before most of the rest of the world even got up. Clean, decent people—the kind that noticed if you came in from the fields with a dirty face and crusted fingers.

Buford and I ate lunch together that day, and he told a little about himself. He said he had been in the Army, had worked around the oil rigs. That was good money, not like this, but his car blew up on him and he had to get back on his feet. He drove truck in the oil fields, but he knew how to do all the roustabout jobs as well.

"You could learn it, too," he said. "Make three times as much as you can make at this."

"How do you get on at a job like that?"

"Aw, hell, you just go up and tell 'em you want to go to work."

"You need to know somethin' about it, don't you?"

He was eating a bologna sandwich, and he brushed away the crumbs from his mouth. "Not much to know. You can learn it as you go along. I could get you on, as far as that goes."

I always wondered why people who could make good money doing something else were working in the fruit fields, but I just said, "Somethin' to think about."

We worked on in the prune orchard for a couple more days, both of us getting sweaty and dirty and making about fifteen dollars a day. Buford rode back and forth with me, and on the fourth day we worked together he gave me another dollar for gasoline.

Then he said, "What would you think if I bought some pork chops, and we cooked 'em up at your place? I can't cook in my room, and I'm kinda tired of eatin' cold food out of a can."

I had already told him what kind of a place I was staying in, and his idea sounded reasonable enough, so I said okay. We went to a grocery store, where he picked out four pork chops, two cans of fruit cocktail, and a loaf of bread. Then at the cash stand he asked for two packs of L&M's. He paid with a five-dollar bill and got two dollars and some change. He asked me if I needed anything else, and I said no.

Back at my place I fried the pork chops, and we ate them along with half a loaf of bread. Then we each had a can of fruit cocktail. It was a simple meal, but it was pretty satisfying, and the swamp cooler had made the place comfortable. Buford pushed back from the little table where we had eaten, lit a cigarette, and dropped the match in an empty fruit can.

"This place isn't too bad," he said. "Do you think it's big enough for two people?"

I shrugged. "I don't know. There's a couple of cabins where two guys stay, but I think they're a little bigger."

"I'll tell ya, I'm only lookin' to stay here for a couple of weeks, and I could sleep on that little couch easy enough. I could give you, say, a dollar a day. That way we'd both come out ahead. Then when I get ready to take off, if you want to go work in the oil fields, I can help you get on. If not, then I'm out of your hair."

"I don't know," I said, looking around.

"Naw, hell," he said. "That's okay. I don't want to crowd you. It's just that I'd rather be givin' money to you than to the folks at the hotel."

I gave it some thought. I could see where he might like to have me go with him to the oil fields, so he could have transportation, at least to get there. And the idea of making more money was a good one to me. On the other hand, if I was going to get tired of this fella, I ought to know it in a week or so, and I could get rid of him just by telling him I didn't feel like moving on.

Meanwhile, a dollar a day was nothing to sneeze at. Everything was on a two-bit scale, it seemed to me. A quart of milk and a loaf of bread both cost two bits. So did a pack of cigarettes. I didn't smoke, but I knew that much. Gas was two bits a gallon or a little more, depending on where you found it. The hourly wage was a dollar and a quarter, and I was averaging a dollar and a half at two bits a box. A dollar a day to have some guy sleeping on my couch for a week or two didn't seem all that bad, and sharing a room was still better than sleeping in my car, which I had done before and might be doing again before long.

"Yeah, why not," I said. "If it doesn't seem like a good idea after a few days, we can go back to doing things like before."

"Oh, hell, yeah," he said as he flicked his ashes in the fruit can. "Last thing I want to do is make a pest of myself. But if it's a go, I can let 'em know at the hotel, and I can take my stuff with me in the mornin'. I'm already paid up for tonight, of course."

"Sure."

"Well, that sounds good, Tom. And I'll tell you, I appreciate it. It's harder'n hell to just get by, and when someone helps you, you remember it."

"It's all right," I said, and I felt pretty good about being able to help out another guy.

* * * * *

He was waiting on the sidewalk the next morning, with a striped pasteboard suitcase next to him and a little traveling bag in his hand. I pulled over to the curb, and he opened the back door and put his belongings inside. Then he got in on the passenger's side of the front seat, and we were off for another day of work.

The early-morning farm program was on the radio, and Webb Pierce was singing "Wonderin'." Buford sang along as he rolled down the window and lit a cigarette. When the song ended he said, "There's somethin' I've been wonderin' about, too." He pronounced it "wanderin'" like the singer did.

"What's that?"

"Why in the hell do they call 'em prunes? I thought prunes was when they were dried, and plums was when they were fresh."

"That's somethin' everyone finds out before long. You've got fresh plums, and you've got fresh prunes. Then when they're dried, they're dried prunes."

"The hell."

"Oh, yeah. These guys that grow 'em, they're particular about it. And you go to work at a dryin' yard, you might find

33

where they've got dried peaches, dried apricots, dried cherries, dried plums, and dried prunes. All of 'em. Whatever you call 'em fresh, that's what you call 'em when they're dried, and vice-versa."

"Well, by God, I never knew any of that."

"I didn't either, at one time."

We rode along for a minute or so until he said, "I've got another question."

"Go ahead."

"The way they're pickin' this fruit with machines, that's pretty new, isn't it?"

"Somewhat. They've been knockin' 'em with machines for quite a few years, but usin' the catch-frames is more recent. Used to be, the knockers would come in and knock enough in a few hours for the crew to pick in one day. Even then, sometimes you had to strip behind the machine, but all the fruit fell on the ground, and the whole family could go to work pickin' it up. Little kids and all. Pickin' up prunes."

"Huh."

Hearing my own voice, I thought about the old song that went, "Dear Okie, if you see Arkie, tell 'im Tex has got a job for him out in California. Pickin' up prunes, squeezin' oil out of olives," but I didn't know how he'd take it. Then "San Antonio Rose" came on the radio, and he started to sing along with it, so I left things at that.

He smoked his cigarette down and flicked the butt out the window. As I saw the sparks in the rear-view mirror, I wondered if he was just trying to make me feel smart.

* * * * *

We worked through that day without much to mention. It was a Friday, and the boss came around in the middle of the afternoon and paid me for everything through noon that day. Then he went to talk to Buford. He seemed to be making the rounds, and he didn't stop to talk very long with either of us.

We cashed our checks at the store where we bought our groceries. I cashed mine first and paid for all the groceries, which the kid in the green apron put in a cardboard box for me. I carried it out to the car and waited as Buford cashed his check and bought a carton of cigarettes. As a general rule I don't look at other people's wallets or money, so I had no interest in knowing how much he had gotten paid. When he came out of the store and climbed into the car, he gave me eight dollars for his half of the groceries.

That evening while he was taking a shower, I put away sixty dollars of my money. In the bottom of my traveling bag, beneath a couple of pairs of folded pants, I had a copy of an old book called *Topper*. It had a dull brown cover with the title of the book, along with the author's name, which I remember was Thorne Smith, in staggered letters across the front. I never read the book, but I remembered seeing parts of the television program, which was a slow-moving comedy about a ghost and odd things that floated on the air. Anyway, I ended up with the book, so I used it as a place to stash money whenever I got a little ahead. Then I dipped into it when I ran low between jobs. I always knew exactly how much I had, so

I didn't have to count it, though I did from time to time. The amount I just put in made two hundred and forty.

When Buford was done with his shower he pulled a chair outside and sat near Slim. He had made friends with the old Cat skinner, and the two of them would sit in the shade and talk as they smoked their cigarettes.

I took a shower and put on my clean clothes, and then as I often did, I went out for an ice cream. Patty was working by herself, as usual. She smiled as she handed me the cone.

The sense of having money stashed away made me feel good about myself, like I wasn't some run-of-the-mill fruit tramp. Still, I didn't think I'd known her long enough to talk about going out, so I just paid her and said, "See you later."

Back at the court, the door was unlocked and the room was empty. I could hear the television going next door, so I figured Buford was watching T.V. with Slim. I checked in my traveling bag, and there was the same old *Topper* with the two hundred and forty dollars safe and sound. I told myself that I was making myself worry, that putting in the sixty dollars hadn't made any big change except to remind me that I had the money hidden there.

* * * * *

We worked Saturday and Sunday just like any other day. When fruit was in season, it was nothing to work thirty days straight, and we were just getting started on this job. Buford plugged right along, working at the same rate as I did. For as much as anyone could have his heart in work like this, he

36

didn't seem to have any feeling for it. He wasn't like the people who hated field work, but as soon as he was out of the orchard he acted as if he had never seen a picking bucket. By the time he had been staying with me for a week, I found myself wishing he would move on. There wasn't anything specific that I disliked—just that he and I weren't on the same wavelength. And he hadn't said much more about Bakersfield and the oil rigs.

One thing did get on my nerves a little, and that was his singing. Once he had gotten familiar with me, he took to singing out loud. I could see that he thought quite a bit of himself in that way. One day he came right out and said it. We had finished eating lunch and were sitting in the shade, and he had just lit a cigarette.

"If I could get the right break," he said, "I could be a singer. A lot of these guys have never had music lessons, much less voice lessons, and look at them. What have they got that I haven't? They got a break somewhere along the way, and now instead of workin' in a truck stop they've got someone drivin' their bus."

I nodded. "Who are you the most like? I mean, if you got to be a big singer, who would you be like?"

His answer came quick. "Webb Pierce."

"Really?"

"People tell me I sound just like him. When I want to. But I can do George Jones, Ray Price—you name it."

"Buck Owens?"

"Sure."

37

I could tell he was serious, and I didn't know enough about any of it to say otherwise. So I asked, "How about 'King of the Road'? Can you do that?"

"You damn right I can." He sat up, stubbed out his cigarette in the dirt clods, and sang that song as if he was Roger Miller himself, dropped down in a prune orchard.

"That was pretty good," I said.

"I just like to sing. If I get the right break some day, maybe you'll hear me on the radio."

* * * * *

On Friday, the boss came around again and paid through noon of that day. With the deductions, my check came out at a hundred and one dollars and some change. When we cashed our checks, Buford gave me eight dollars for room rent and five for gas, so I put an even hundred in with the rest of my hoard. Buford was in the shower, so I took the time to count the bills. It was all there.

After we ate, he went over to Slim's to watch T.V., and I got cleaned up and went to the Frostie stand. I'd been there only once during the week, and I hoped the girl was glad to see me. She seemed like maybe she was. She smiled as she took my order and then handed me the cone.

As I paid her I asked, "Do you ever get tired of workin' all the time?"

"Sometimes, but there's not much else to do."

"Do you ever go out?"

"Once in a while."

My heartbeat picked up, and I was afraid of saying the wrong thing, so I just asked, "Where do you go?"

"Depends."

"Depends on . . . "

"Depends on who it is and what they want to do, and whether I can do it."

"Like whether it's bowling or the drive-in?"

"I can't go to the drive-in because it's out of town."

"Oh." I noticed the ice cream was starting to slip, and I didn't want to lick it right in front of her. "Well," I said, "there's no law against me askin' you next week, is there?"

"No, but I don't work Monday, you know."

"I remember that. So what if I come by on Tuesday?"

"No law against that."

Back at the room, Buford was still watching T.V. next door, and all my money was just as I left it. I sat around and killed time, thinking about how I was going to ask the girl to go out with me.

Buford came back at about nine. "Might as well turn in," he said. "Day starts early tomorrow."

We went through the same routine as every night except that now, just before I pulled the string on the overhead light, I noticed something for the first time. He had a tattoo on his right ankle. It looked like a row of numbers, nothing fancy, not like a girl's name that some guys had on their arm or shoulder. I thought he caught me looking at it, but then I shut out the light and neither of us said anything.

* * * * *

We went to work the next day, and everything seemed like normal. At a little before noon, Buford was gone for a while, like he'd been to the outhouse at the end of the orchard, and he came back.

"Say," he called as I was setting a lug box on the stack. "This old boy and his kid are goin' into town for a few minutes and then comin' back. They said I could go along. I need to wire some money to my brother, and the Western Union might be closed later on."

"Your brother?" This was the first time he had ever talked about any family.

"Yeah. My twin brother. I don't think I'll be gone more'n an hour."

I shrugged. As long as he didn't ask me to take him in, I wasn't going to lose any time. "Go ahead," I said. "I'll help you get caught up on your row when you get back." That was no skin off my ass either, because everything I picked would go into my box and get marked with a forty-nine in blue chalk. I looked at his stack, with the numbers all written in yellow orange, and I thought, I really couldn't worry about how much he made.

I worked on through the afternoon, and he didn't show up. I thought I heard that other car come back, and doors slamming at the edge of the orchard, so when I found a good stopping place I walked over a couple of rows and down toward the end where I could hear the man and his kid whacking branches and plunking fruit in a bucket.

The old man didn't have much to tell me. He said Buford offered him five dollars to take him to town, and when they got there, Buford asked him to leave him off at the cabin court. And that was it. I didn't know what to make of that, so I went back to my row. I picked a couple of more boxes, and then it got to eatin' on me, so I went to find the boss.

He was just turning into the orchard, driving a tractor and pulling an empty trailer with two swampers sitting on it, smoking cigarettes. He stepped on the clutch, cut the throttle, and tossed his head in a question.

"I was wondering if you knew what was up with this other guy, Buford," I said.

He shook his head. "I don't know. Why?"

"He went into town, and I thought he was coming back."

"I don't know. I thought he rode with you."

"He did. But he caught a ride with this guy and his kid."

"That's more than I know. I hope he doesn't go on a drunk."

"Well," I said, "I think I'm done for the day anyway. I guess I'll find out when I get back to town."

* * * * *

When I went into the room, I knew right away. Nothing was out of place, but all of his stuff was gone, and the key I had gotten for him was sitting on the dresser. I felt a sinking in my gut as I reached down by the far side of the bed and hauled up my traveling bag. I reached under the folded pants and brought out the old brown copy of *Topper*. I turned to the

41

back cover, where I had always tucked the bills, and it was as bare as the front.

A hopeless, empty feeling set in as I held the book in my hand. This was what a person got, I thought. Try to go straight, help someone else, and they play you for a chump.

I didn't feel like eating or taking a shower or doing a damn thing, but I made myself eat a can of sardines and a couple of slices of bread. Then I went outside to tell my story to Slim.

He didn't seem surprised. "You can bet one thing," he said. "That bird's long gone. You just don't know which way."

He was right. The busses ran north and south through this town, a couple of times a day each way.

I shook my head. "What a son of a bitch. Said he had to send money to his twin brother. And then he does this." I was having a hard time with the whole idea, like I was falling and hadn't stopped yet.

"It's just the kind of guy he is. He'll probably piss it away, then go on to the next place."

"I'd like to know where that was."

Slim made a little spitting sound. "That's another thing you can bet. You'll never see him again."

"I imagine." But I knew I'd be on the lookout for him everywhere I went. "There's one thing I was wonderin' about," I said.

"What's that?"

"Do they put a tattoo on your ankle when you're in the Army?"

"Not that I know of. Why?"

"This guy had one there."

"Ohhhh...." said Slim. "They do that in the joint. And unless he was in the Army first, that would have kept him out."

"So that was probably just another lie. All I was was a patsy for him."

"Well, I'm sorry for you, kid. But things like this are supposed to teach us somethin'. Help you learn to paddle your own canoe. Make you tough, help you get back on top."

Get back on top. It was like a capsized canoe and my hands kept slipping. "It doesn't feel that way."

"Not yet."

I shook my head again and tried to pull in a deep breath. I knew that as much as anything, it was the idea that the guy had gone into my room, reached into my bag, and opened that book—probably not the first time, either. And I had trusted him. "It's like I've been walked all over," I said.

"Look, kid, I know this is easy for me to say, but you need to get the best of this thing. Look at it this way. You've still got a job and a way to get there. As for this other money, it's shot in the ass. You're never goin' to see it again, or that cheap bastard either. Just start over."

I knew he was right, but I also knew I couldn't make myself feel a certain way. I was just going to have to get through it. There was one thing I could do, one thing I knew how to do. I could go back to work alone and look out for myself. No one else was going to do it for me.

Killing for Chocolate

During the summer I met Faustina, stories drifted through the labor camps about street girls disappearing from one town and another in the valley. I never knew of any girls who sold it in the camps, but I heard about it from men who went to town on payday. I went along one time myself, but I wasn't interested in that kind of action, so I stayed in the car. I saw the girls who worked the streets. At the camp in the evenings and in the fields during the day, I heard about others—girls who worked the bars, girls who served drinks, girls who dealt cards. The guys referred to them by name or by nickname, in Spanish and in English, and I never thought of them as being from our way of life. They were town girls, who lived by night, and when the talk came around about one of them disappearing, it didn't seem like anything that happened to us.

Faustina wasn't a street girl. She worked in the fields with her family. She wasn't pure and innocent, though. She had done it with other guys before I met her, and she may have been doing it with others when she was seeing me. Actually, toward the end, I know she was. But I never held it against her.

She was a pretty girl, in a plain way. She had a dark complexion with smooth, clear skin. She had dark eyes with long eyelashes, and when she had showered in the evening, her black hair tumbled to her shoulders. Also in the evening she wore short-sleeve blouses and light-colored pants. She was in good shape from doing field work, and it hadn't made her look rough at all. She looked soft and firm at the same time, and after she had a shower, she looked fresh. Not that she looked bad in her work clothes, but when she was cleaned up, she made a fellow think that life might have something good in store for him after all.

When I met her, we were staying in the same camp. It was run by a labor contractor named Jim Jaconetti. The first time I heard his name, I thought it was three people—Jim, Jack, and Eddie. But it was all the same person. He didn't own the two labor camps or any of the fields we worked in. He just ran things and got his percentage. As far as I knew, the only things he owned were the faded red Ford Falcon Ranchero that he used for work and the black Oldsmobile Toronado that he drove in the evening. I don't think he owned the trailer house he lived in.

The camp where I met Faustina was like some of the government camps, only smaller. It consisted of two rows of houses with sheet metal walls and roofs, cement floors, and plastic windows. Each house was a duplex, and the bathrooms were outside. There was never much privacy in a labor camp, but people could find ways to slip off and do things if they wanted. So Faustina and I agreed to meet, and I picked her up in my old Packard. We kissed, and I felt her soft round boobs, and I got my hand inside her blouse and pants. Then the pants came down, and I saw her brown mid-section and dark slope, and in another minute her brown body was pushing against my white one as we sweated in the rough cloth upholstery of my car.

On the third night we met, she said, "I wish we could do this every night."

"And not in the back seat of a car," I said. I took a little courage. "We could go away and be together."

"Could we really do that?"

"We can if we want," I said. "Work together and keep at it, get out of this life."

I believed it. I thought we could make it on our own, and I believed that she wanted to. For two weeks, we would meet for a little while every night, and we would talk about what we could do on our own. It all seemed real at the time. Even now, after I've had so long to think about it, I believe it was something she meant for at least as long as she was with me.

For those two weeks and a little more, we worked on the same crew in the tomato fields. That year was one of the first that they had mechanical harvesters, and the machinery broke down so much that the growers got way behind. The crops were ripening and on the brink of going to waste, so the farmers went back to picking by hand. They got Jim Jaconetti to put together the crews and get them into the fields.

We worked by the bucket. Each person had a row and picked into five-gallon black buckets, the kind that harvester grease came in. The work was stoop labor, unless a person wanted to kneel between the furrows where the overripe tomatoes had already fallen off. We picked the good fruit, not the mushy stuff and not the green ones, so we left a lot of waste. When I filled my two buckets I took them to the wagon, called out my number, and dumped the buckets into a bin. It was hot, miserable work, out in an open field with the temperature over a hundred. The smell of warm tomatoes hung everywhere. My hands were caked with dirt that stuck to the tomato juice and to the green smudge that rubbed off from the vines. But it wasn't all bad. From time to time I caught a look from Faustina, and that kept my spirits up.

As we finished one field and then another, Jim moved people around. One day he came up to me and said, "I'm puttin' you on the other crew. You and two other guys. When you get back to the camp after work, get your stuff ready. I'll come by at about seven, and you can follow me to the other camp."

I just looked at him. There he was, in a clean cap and a clean checkered shirt, dealing with us like we were so many cattle. He wore sunglasses, like some row bosses and owners did, and he had a dark mustache and dark, hairy arms. He had a pen and a notepad in his shirt pocket, but he didn't write our checks. I didn't see where he was that high above us, except that he had the power to hire and fire and boss us around.

When I didn't answer, he said, "You're Merrill, aren't you?"

"Yeah."

"Well, be ready at seven."

I ended up in a place ten miles from Faustina. It was an old prune-picking camp, close to the river where the mosquitoes were worse. The houses were old, rundown shacks with tin roofs and screen windows. I shared a house with the two young Okies who got moved along with me, guys about my age in their early twenties.

For the next several days when I got back from the field and washed up, I drove my Packard to Faustina's camp. I was always anxious to see her and in a hurry to get going. My stomach was nervous, and I would drum my fingers on the steering wheel as I kept my foot on the gas.

It would have been bad enough if I was just hooked on the sex. But we had plans. We were going to go off together, work our way up out of that life, and make something of ourselves. We would have our own house, not have to move every time a job ended. And we would have jobs that lasted. I was hooked on her and on the idea of what we were going to do, and I didn't want it to slip away from me.

That made it rough when I went to her camp one night and her brother said she wasn't there. He wouldn't tell me where she was. I waited in my car, paced up and down the camp, and sat in my car again. It was way after dark when I went home.

All the next day I had an empty, hopeless feeling. No matter how hard I pushed myself, I could feel the worry eating away on me. Every time I emptied my buckets I looked at the end of the field. I day-dreamed that she would have someone drive her here—maybe her brother, maybe Jim Jaconetti—and she would make things right. But of course she never came.

That night she was at home. She came out of her house and talked to me, but she seemed a mile away. I was dying to touch her, but if I moved toward her she moved away.

"I guess you don't want me anymore," she said.

"Of course I do. I want you more than ever. I wish we could go away now."

Her eyes were troubled as she shook her head. "We can't."

"I know."

She looked away and said nothing.

"What's wrong?" I asked. "Did something happen?"

"It's just that you're so far away."

"Do you forget about me?"

"No." She drew the word out.

"Then what is it?"

"I don't know. Maybe I'm just no good."

"Of course you are. Especially when you're with me. We're going to get out of all of this, be better than it."

"I know you want to."

"Don't you?"

She looked down. "Of course I do. I hate it more than you do."

"We could go away now," I said.

"No," she said. "Like we talked about. When the work's over."

I felt lost, as if everything was out of my reach. "Won't you come with me tonight?" I asked.

"Not tonight."

"Why not?"

"I don't know. I guess I feel—dirty."

I looked her over. "You're not dirty. You're clean and you're beautiful, and you'll always be that way with me." I took her hand. "Come with me tonight. Please."

She gave me a painful look, and again she seemed a mile away. "Not tonight. I can't."

"When, then?"

"Tomorrow. I'll work all day tomorrow, and they won't be mad at me anymore."

"Didn't you work today?"

"Please, Stevie. I don't want to talk about it."

"Will you see me tomorrow, then?"

"Come back tomorrow. Things will be better."

For a second night I didn't sleep worth a damn. I tossed and turned, got up to drink water, got up to take a leak. When I did fall asleep, it seemed like ten minutes later when I heard people in the camp getting up and starting the day.

I had so much nervous energy that I could have moved a barn, but all I had was my two buckets and a row of cannery tomatoes. I threw myself at the work and tried to wear myself out, but I stayed on edge as the day dragged on.

Several miles away I could see a cluster of tall, dark trees. It was the way things were done in the big farms in the valley, to set the headquarters in the center of the whole operation with fields all around. In that grove of trees there would be a house, a barn, a garage, and other sheds. Inside the house, the air would be cool, and whoever was there would have a television and a refrigerator. Maybe even a color television. There was probably a green lawn where people sat on chairs in the evening. I wondered how close I would ever come to that kind of life, and I wondered how long, if at all, Faustina would go along with me.

That evening she went with me in the car, and everything was like before. Her soft brown mid-section rose to meet me, touched and lowered, rose again. I told her I loved her, whispering but not very quiet. It was as if we had always done this and always would, yet at the same time I felt desperate. I had the fear that we would never be together again.

But we were. The next night was more of the same, but maybe more magical than ever. Her dark slope with the black, wiry hair took me in and held me, all of me inside her, as if I had gone out of myself and blended with her. Faustina and I were one, and we would always be together.

The next night I fell hard. Her brother told me she wasn't at home, and he wouldn't tell me why. I was stunned, as if I had been slammed to the ground, and at the same time I felt as if I was falling down a dark hole and never hit the bottom.

My mind was swirling. I felt more lost than ever. I paced up and down, drank from the water faucet, sat in my car, paced some more. Two middle-aged Mexican guys were sitting in a '56 Buick and drinking from a bottle in a brown paper bag. I knew them from when I had stayed at the camp, and I didn't care for either of them, but I went over to their car when they called.

The one behind the wheel was a guy named Pross. He spoke pretty good English. He offered me the bottle, which was a fifth of muscatel. After I took a drink, he said, "You worried about that girl, huh?"

I took a deep breath. "I guess so. I don't know what to think."

"Those girls are always trouble," he said. "They want one guy, then they want another. They want more."

"She's not that way," I said.

He shrugged. "Thass okay. You crazy about her. But you're young. You get over it."

"What do you mean? Do you think she's done with me?"

As he handed me the bottle again, he said, "She wants more."

"You mean someone else besides me, or more than me?"

"More than you can give her."

"Oh, I don't think so."

He shrugged again. "You mean you hope. But thass okay."

I let the warmth of the muscatel spread through my mouth, throat, and chest. "Do you know who she goes out with?"

"I think so."

"Why don't you tell me? It's drivin' me crazy."

"It won't make nothin' any better."

"Oh, just tell me, won't you?"

"Sure. I tell you." And he said the name, pronounced it as if it was three people.

* * * * *

I know my mind wasn't right after that. I couldn't sleep at night, and I couldn't sit still for five minutes when I should have been getting rest in the evening. On some nights I didn't leave my own camp, but on most nights I went to her camp. Whether she was there or not, her brother said she wasn't at home. He told me that once, and I saw her walking back from the bathrooms with a towel over her arm. Her hair was washed and hanging loose, and she looked as clean as could be. It tore me to pieces to see her like that, so close but out of reach, and she wouldn't look my way.

One night I went to her camp three times. Pross just shook his head and gave me a look that said, "I told you so."

I started spending some of the money I had rat-holed. It cost me to drive back and forth, and it cost me to drink cheap whiskey to try to get some sleep.

Of course, when I had something to drink I had friends. Two of them were the ones I shared the house with. I smoked their cigarettes and they drank my booze.

Three others were young pachuco types from Texas. They told stories about how the wetbacks sneaked across the border and about stealing a car and driving it a hundred miles an hour. From one of them, a guy named Freddie, I bought a short-barreled .38 and a box of shells. He said it wasn't hot, but I knew better. It cost me an even hundred, so the money I had stashed away for me and Faustina was going fast. Freddie and his pals went out to the levee with me, and I learned to shoot the .38 at beer bottles. Every time I hit one, the other guys would laugh like hell.

Freddie was a sleaze, and so were his buddies, but they knew their way around. They knew where the street girls hung out, and they knew where Jim Jaconetti lived. I didn't want to have anything to do with those girls, but one night when they mentioned Jim's place, I said, hell, yes, let's cruise by and see where he lives.

He had a trailer house on a piece of gravelly ground where nothing but star thistles grew. It was out on the west side of the valley, where the houses were scattered apart. The lights were off and his dull red Ranchero was parked in front, so I figured he was out for the night.

When we got back from our cruise, I left Freddie and the other two and drove to Faustina's camp.

Her brother came out of the house and told me she didn't want to see me anymore.

"I don't believe it," I said.

"You better believe it."

"I want to hear it from her."

He shook his head.

"I want to know if she's here." I could hear my voice, loud. It sounded outside of me, and I imagined he could smell the liquor on my breath.

"Just go," he said, and he walked back into the house.

The next day, Jim Jaconetti called me aside after I dumped my two buckets in the wagon. It was about four o'clock, and I was hot and tired. The thick smell of tomatoes hung in the air and mixed with the tractor fumes as the diesel engine idled. I waited as Jim took out a cigarette, rapped it on his lighter, and lit it. He pushed out his chest as he blew the smoke away.

"You can go back to the camp now," he said. "I'll get your tally and bring your check by later."

I looked at his dark glasses and didn't see much. "You mean I'm fired?"

"I'm lettin' a few people go," he said.

"What for?"

"It's how I manage my crews." He raised his dark, hairy arm and paused with the cigarette at his lips. "You can leave your buckets at the wagon."

Back at the camp later on, I asked Freddie if Jim had fired anyone else from the crew, and he said he didn't know of any. So I doubted that Jim saw us drive by his place the night before. I figured he was firing me for the scene I caused when I went to her camp.

After I got fired, I kept to myself. I lived in the car for a few days and then rented a room in a cabin court. I got a job picking melons, where we started at six and knocked off at three. After I ate and got cleaned up each night, I went on a drive. I would get a bottle of whiskey and park a mile away from his trailer in one direction or another. As I sat in the dark I would see headlights of cars going off to who-knows-where. When I saw his lights head into his place, I would wait a while and then drive by. There I would see his Toronado parked next to the Ranchero. Sometimes the lights were on in the trailer, and sometimes they were off. But I never timed it to where I would see him go in or come out, and I never knew for sure if had her with him.

Until one night. It had been more than a week since that night I went to Faustina's labor camp, but I drove past it from time to time, and on this evening I saw the black Toronado pull out onto the two-lane and drive away ahead of me. I couldn't see who was in the car, but I thought of a way of finding out. With my nerves jangled as usual, I drove in to the camp. I saw Pross before I saw anyone else, so I pulled up next to his car and left my motor running as I leaned out the window.

"Do you know if she's here?" I asked.

He shrugged and shook his head.

"I just want to know, one way or another. It's eatin' me up."

"It won't do you no good to know."

"Just tell me. I'll worry about the rest."

He stalled for a few seconds and said, "Well, she ain't here."

"How long ago did she leave?"

"Just before you got here."

"Thanks." I ground my car into gear and pulled out of there with my tires crunching in the gravel.

Out on the pavement I floored it, and the old Packard took right off. I got out to Jim Jaconetti's neighborhood just as his brake lights went off. A second later his headlights died, and a minute after that the lights went on in the trailer.

I parked about a mile away from his place and sat in my car, fidgeting. I didn't have a bottle with me that night. Every three or four minutes I would light a match and look at my watch, and I couldn't believe how slow the time crawled by. After an hour I got out and walked toward the trailer.

I had the gun with me, of course, and I had it loaded. On top of that, I had seventeen shells that I hadn't burned up on empty bottles. The shells were loose in my pants pocket. I didn't have any idea of what I would do with that many bullets, but then again I didn't have a plan even for the gun.

The light was still on in the front of the trailer, and nothing had changed since I first parked. The night was warm, and I walked along in my t-shirt with the .38 in one pocket and the cartridges rattling in the other. As I got closer to the trailer, I put my hand on the outside of my pocket to stop the noise.

The trailer house was situated perpendicular to the road. The Ford Ranchero was parked in front of the nose of the trailer, and the Toronado sat to the left of the Ford. The wooden steps weren't more than twenty feet from either car.

My heart was beating fast as I stood by the tail end of the Ranchero and listened. I thought I heard footsteps inside, but I couldn't be sure. Then the outdoor light came on, and I felt a jolt in the pit of my stomach. I ducked down on the right side of the Ford.

Jim Jaconetti came out of the trailer house by himself. I heard a jangle of keys, then the sound of a car trunk opening. I rose up enough to see him go back into the house. A minute later, he came out with a bundle wrapped in a sheet. My heart was pounding hard when I stood up and saw a head of dark hair at one end of the bundle and a brown ankle and foot sticking out the other end.

He dumped her in the trunk like a sack of onions, and before he closed the lid he turned and looked around. He was an average-sized guy, maybe 5'10", with square shoulders and a full head of hair. He wasn't wearing his cap or his dark glasses. He had a strange expression on his face as he looked out into the night, as if he hated anybody or anything that might see him.

I hated him, too. I got a steady aim across the bed of the Ranchero, pulled the trigger, and put a .38 slug in his chest. He jerked back, and his hand hit the open trunk lid and sent it bobbing. I came around the back of the Ranchero as he was trying to stand up straight. He had one hand on the back bumper and one hand on the tail light. I shot him two more times in the body, and when he hit the ground I stood over him to see if I needed to shoot him again. I didn't.

I looked into the trunk and saw Faustina slumped where she had landed, with the sheet falling away from her face and from her legs. I sat on the ground and cried, and I was still sitting there when the cops came.

* * * * *

The first days were the worst, when I knew I would never see Faustina again and could never make anything right with anybody. I knew I had lost everything, thrown it all away—what little I had, and whatever I hoped to be. Then the process set in. The public defender had me plead not guilty, but the district attorney had all the evidence in the world to prove motive, means, and premeditation. I would meet with my public defender, and he would go talk to the others. A few days later, he would come back to talk to me. In the end I took a deal and got life.

Before I took the deal, I learned something that wouldn't have changed anything but gave me more to think about. When the cops found out that Faustina died from choking, Jim Jaconetti became a suspect in the missing street girls. Six of them disappeared that summer. The main thing the cops had to go on was the testimony of one girl who had gotten away when a man of his description tried to choke her in the back seat of a black Toronado. Their other evidence was that the street girls quit disappearing. This was in 1966, and there wasn't any such thing as surveillance tapes and DNA evidence then, but the cops were pretty sure of their man. Still, they were pissed at me for barging in and ruining things, because they never got to question him about where he hid the bodies.

A year later, five girls were found buried in an abandoned gravel pit seven or eight miles from his trailer. The cops were able to identify them all and match them up with girls who had gone missing. One was colored, two were Mexican, one was Filipino, and one was white. They were all buried naked, just as Faustina would have been.

* * * * *

That was a long time ago. From the night they arrested me to the day I got out on parole, I spent thirty-eight years, seven months, and twenty-three days behind bars. I went in a young man of twenty-two and came out a broken-down, grey-haired man of sixty with a jailhouse complexion.

The world was different, way different. I had seen it on television, but it was even more different in real life. Everybody knew everything and had a right to say anything they wanted. An average fool on the street could go on television and say absurd things about the president. Everyone was a comedian and an expert on pro sports and a whiz with a cell phone.

After I got a job and a car, which took some time in itself, I took a drive one day. I don't think it was the famous urge to return to the scene of the crime as much as to visit the place where I saw Faustina for the last time.

That whole side of the valley was full of expensive acreages with country homes and white rail fences. The place where Jim Jaconetti's trailer had sat now had a house with brick facing, a circular drive, and a horse barn. From there I drove west to the place where the old gravel pit had been. The hole had been filled in, and a moving and storage company occupied the place. But to my eyes, there was no covering up what that one man had caused.

I shouldn't begrudge these know-it-all modern people with their cell phones and G.P.S. devices. I work with them where I stock shelves, and I hear the things they say— thoughtless things so far from reality in a world of reality t.v. and spill-your-guts talk shows. "My parents are going to kill me when they find out," one kid says. Or another says, "So right next to me there's this car that I would kill for." Then the comedian. "Chocolate. Oh, my God, I just *love* chocolate. I could kill for chocolate."

It makes me want to tell them what killing a person comes to. I want to tell them there's nothing funny about killing for chocolate. But deeper down, I don't want to talk to them at all. I think of how Faustina never got a chance in life and how that guy must have thought he had a right to do what he did. Every time I think of how he came out of that trailer with her wrapped in a sheet and how he looked around after he dumped her in the trunk of his car, I know I would do it all again.

At the End of the Orchard

One of the biggest lies I heard in the fruit fields, and I heard it often enough, was that the picking was better at the other end of the orchard. The fruit was just hangin' on the trees, all of it sized up. After a few times, a guy just thought, yeah, yeah, it's always better at the other end, and he went ahead and picked whatever trees came his way. But at the Sagers place, the time I worked there, it was worse than the regular lie. What was at the end of the orchard that time wasn't any good for anyone.

The job seemed normal enough when I first went out. Al Sagers was sitting in his pickup between two rows of picked trees. The GMC was a few years old, maybe a 1960 or '61, and it had a "Goldwater for President" sticker on the back bumper. When I pulled off the road and parked at the edge of the trees, the boss got out, stood by the cab, and waited.

"Labor office sent me out," I said as I walked toward him. "Said you needed pickers."

"By yourself?"

"Yeah."

"Well, I need some. We're just three days into the season, and the fruit isn't ripening very fast. Things pick up, I'll need some more, but I could do with one or two right now."

"They said you've got a camp."

He was wearing dark glasses and standing in the shade, so I couldn't see his eyes, but as his head moved up and down I could tell he was looking me over. "I've got some tent cabins left. If things get full up, you might have to share it, but you can have one to yourself for right now." He took in a breath and stood up straight, the kind of guy who used his height to help him be the boss. "Follow me," he said. "I'll show you where it is."

* * * * *

Mine was the second in a row of five cabins, wood-framed with canvas covering. It sat on a wooden platform and was wired for one overhead light bulb inside. I got my stuff moved in and gave the place a once-over. Twelve by twelve, it looked like. I hoped I didn't have to share it.

Sitting in the doorway, I could look up and down and see the whole labor camp. Across the way sat a row of four older wooden houses, with the bathrooms in a separate building between the second and third house. The tent cabins were only a couple of years old, but the houses had to be at least thirty.

A parking area of bare, packed dirt, about fifty feet across, lay between the two rows of shacks. At the left end of that stretch, as I glanced around, stood an old barn. I was gazing at that when I heard a car coming into camp. It was a dark green Oldsmobile, about a '54, and it parked in front of the third house. Another car came in, and then two more. Car doors opened and closed, and people went into the houses. A couple of minutes later, a girl with blond hair and pale legs came out of the third house and went into the bathroom. It was the most interesting thing I'd seen all day, so I loafed around until I saw her come out about fifteen minutes later, carrying a towel I hadn't noticed before. That was the thing about peaches. Everyone wanted to wash off the itchy fuzz as soon as they could.

I got antsy just sitting there, so I decided to get up and stretch my legs. I was hoping to catch that girl's eye as well. I strolled out to the driveway and down to the old barn. The entryway had no doors on it, so anyone could look in and not be snooping. When I did, I saw an assortment of dusty old prop boards, battered picking buckets, knocking poles for some crop like prunes or almonds, and dilapidated ladders with missing steps and broken legs. Not much to see there.

I went back to sit in my doorway, smoke a cigarette, and wait for another change in scenery. I hadn't been there very long when a soft-looking fellow came meandering by and stopped.

"Hi, there," he said. "New, huh?"

"Yeah. How's the pickin'?"

He shrugged and took out a pack of Salems. "About normal." He tipped the pack, and a cigarette slid down into his palm. He lit it with a tin Zippo, then snapped the lighter shut. "Name's Bud."

"Oh, uh-huh. Mine's Charlie."

He looked at my car, then back at me. "Where you been working?"

He struck me as a busy-body, but I was pretty sure he came out of the same house as the blond girl, so I gave him a straight answer. "In the apricots. Down in Winters. How about yourself?"

"Huh. Well, we been here since May, me 'n' my daughter."

"May?"

"Yeah. Thinning peaches. Then the green drop after that—you know, when they knock whatever percentage they agree not to harvest."

"Oh, yeah." Maybe that was what the poles were for. "And you've stayed on since then?"

"Well, after that I wangled a job with Al working around the camp. You know, small repairs on the houses, fix ladders, keep down the weeds, and answer questions to anyone who pulls in. It don't pay much, but the rent's free, and when you come right down to it, most of what you make on any job gets eaten up just tidin' you over until you can get paid at the next place. So I'm getting by all right, not havin' to move or pay rent."

"Sure."

"I live in the third house there, just to the left of the bathrooms. Al said we might have to move into a tent if he got a family in here that needed the house. I'm hopin' not."

I nodded. All the time I was listening to him, I was thinking how much I'd like to get next to his daughter, and he didn't make me like him enough that I would feel guilty for thinking that way.

He didn't strike me as the kind of guy who was going to pick many peaches, either. I didn't want to know any more of his story than I had to, and I thought that if I heard very much, it wouldn't hold together very well. But he stayed long enough to finish his cigarette, and then he went back to his place.

My impression of him stayed about the same the next evening when I talked to the other white man in the camp. He lived in the first house with his large-boned wife and two boys. His name was Jack Horton, and after the first day I worked he sent one of the boys over to invite me to eat with them. He was a real fruit tramp, not just marking time. He drank Gallo port from a brown paper bag and smoked his Pall Malls down to a thin snipe. As the wife and kids cleaned up the dishes, he crouched on the floor in a fruit-picker's squat, with the ash tray and wine bottle in front of him, and squinted through the smoke as he talked.

I mentioned meeting Bud, the man with the daughter.

Jack sniffed. "Yeah, he says he's her father. I'd say step-father at best, and I doubt that girl's of age." He pressed the paper bag around the neck of the bottle. "Course, who's gonna say anything around here? Sure not the boss, the way this guy's kissed his ass."

"Huh. I wonder what she thinks about it."

"Probably not much. She's one of those that was standin' behind the door when the brains got passed out."

* * * * *

The way the picking went, the crew took four rows through the orchard, with the wagon going down the drive in the middle. Partway through the first morning, I had a tree next to Bud and his daughter, and I caught her eye a couple of times.

I thought I saw something there, not very bright but maybe crafty. I saw it again the next day, too, and though I didn't exchange a word with her, I did catch her name. Bud called her Cricket.

I noticed that Jack and his boys didn't gab with anyone else. They kept to themselves, picked their trees, and moved right along. Bud and his daughter, meanwhile, piddled around and got behind, so sometimes one or both of the Salazar boys would have to help them catch up.

The Salazars were from Texas, like the other Mexican family and a lot of others I met. The old man kept them in line. The two older boys, around eighteen, worked on ladders like their father did, and the two girls, fourteen and fifteen or so, picked bottoms and stood around and complained about the heat and the mosquitoes. The five of them took a set of two trees at a time, and since they were the fastest working, they would get called on to help out Bud and the girl. And besides, it looked like one Salazar boy had eyes for Cricket.

I don't think I would have been as interested in her if I was in any place better than a lousy peach orchard. But out there, she was the one thing that looked like a possibility. The two Salazar girls were too young, jail bait for sure. The other two girls, from the Vásquez family, were way out of reach.

Toni and Lupe, somewhere in the eighteen-to-nineteen-year-old range, started out picking with their father, Juan, and their younger brother, Rubén. After a couple of days, Al put them on as sorters, so they worked one on each side of the wagon, tossing out anything green, undersized, or rotten. They were hard, silent girls, both of them. They wore straw hats, scarves, long-sleeved shirts, gloves, and baggy pants. I could tell they were proud and ashamed, and they wanted to keep out any traces of working in the fields. They spoke to no one—not Al when he came around at mid-morning in his sunglasses and clean shirt, not Bud when he tried to make small talk, and certainly not me, just a nameless fruit tramp who called out his number when he stepped onto the running board and dumped his peaches into the bin with the rest.

The checker, who kept a tally of how many buckets each person picked, was a man named Chano. He was a single man in his early thirties, from Mexico. He wasn't related to anyone else on the crew, so he was a good one to be a checker. He was always clean and well-shaven, and he smiled and whistled and sang all day long. He said he wanted to be a professional singer. Whether he would ever make it I don't know, but he wasn't likely to be working in the fields all his life. He was a smooth one. The Vásquez girls didn't talk to him either.

After a couple of days on the crew, I could sit in my doorway and have everyone placed as if we had all lived there for years. Jack Horton with his wife and kids took up the first house; Juan Vásquez and family lived in the second; skip the bathrooms, and you came to the house where Bud and Cricket stayed; and in the last house, the Salazars overflowed. On my side, Chano had the first tent while I had the second. Three more were empty, but the way the talk ran, Al was going to bring in a bunch of people and put on a second crew as soon as the fruit was ready. That might mean Bud and Cricket having to move, or me sharing the tent with some other single guy. However it worked, none of it was going to last very long.

In the evening, the two Salazar boys, all scrubbed up, went out and sat in their '59 Chevy and listened to the radio with the doors opened. The two girls cackled and talked loud, just as they did when they were lolly-gagging in the orchard. On my second evening in camp, when I was in the bathroom shaving, I heard them giggling with the Horton boys and sing-songing. One of the poems went:

> When I die, bury me,
> Hang my balls in a cherry tree,
> When they're ripe, take a bite,
> I hope they taste like dynamite.

Then they broke out laughing and shrieking. I hadn't heard girls that young talk that way before.

Once in a while Bud would wander around and talk, but most of the time he was holed up indoors before dark. On the second evening, when I walked past his screen door, I saw him sitting on a wooden chair in front of a small, black, square-edged, metal t.v. that flickered black and white. When I was back sitting in the doorway of my tent, I saw Cricket's light-colored shape going out to the bathroom. Her blond hair was almost white, and the shorts she wore around camp gave a flash of her legs.

I finally talked to her the third night I was there. I had just finished taking a shower, and as I came out damp and clean into the warm air, I saw her loitering by the corner of her house.

"Hi," I said. "Your name's Cricket, isn't it?"

"Yeah." She was chewing gum. "What's yours?"

"Charlie."

"That's your car, huh?"

I looked at my '56 Plymouth, which wasn't much. "Oh, yeah."

"Where do you go in it?"

"Anywhere I want." Which was a lie, and I knew it as I said it.

She rolled her head. "Oh, I just get tired of this place. I wish I could go out and get some fresh air."

"Just cruise down the highway, huh? With the windows down."

She gave me a sliding look. "Yeah."

I motioned with my head toward her house, and real low I said, "Does he let you go out?"

"I can go out." She lowered her voice. "I can go through the orchard and be out on the road, if I want to."

I perked up. "Tonight?"

She nodded.

* * * * *

I did it with her in the back seat of my Plymouth that night. She was waiting by the road, and when I stopped she jumped in. I found a canal bank, and ten minutes later she was lifting her hips as I pulled her shorts down. That's when I noticed her stomach was swelling. It didn't stop me, of course, and if anything it assured me I wasn't going to knock her up.

It was over pretty quick, and then there wasn't much to say or do. I asked her if Bud was really her father.

"Yeah, he's my real dad. Why?"

"Oh, nothin', really. It's just that he's got dark hair, and yours is light."

"Mine would be darker, but I keep it this way."

"Oh." Now that I thought of it, she was light brown in the spot I had just seen.

"How about you?"

"What about me?"

"Have you always been single?"

"Oh, yeah."

"Do you ever think you'd rather not be, so you could have this every night if you wanted?"

"Well, I guess I don't think about that very much— about, um, not being single."

"You just want to take what you can get, huh? And then leave?"

"Not really . . . ."

"What's wrong with me, then?"

"What do you mean?"

"You could have it any time you wanted. Just like now. I didn't put up any fight at all. And if we were married, it would be yours, just like that." She snapped her fingers.

I got scared. "That's fine," I said. "But look, I think it's a big jump, to marry someone just because you did it once."

A funny look came into her eye, like she wasn't all there. "That's easy for you to say. You got what you want, and now you're done. I was good enough to do it with, but not good enough for anything else. You're all the same. Good talkers and you get what you want." Then her voice took on a sarcastic tone, like she was imitating someone, even though she sounded like a moron. "Play your cards right, and you could be ridin' around in a nice car."

"I didn't say that. I didn't try to trick you into anything. I just thought we both wanted to do the same thing."

"You got what you wanted, that's what. You're all the same."

I figured whoever put the bun in her oven had given her a pretty good line, and I was glad it wasn't me. "Look," I said. "If I thought you were going to expect that of me—"

"I don't expect anything." She sulked for a few seconds and then, not sounding so mad, she said, "Can I have a cigarette?"

"Sure." I shook out a Winston for her and lit a match.

"Thanks. You can take me home now."

We both got into the front seat, and I figured that was about it with this girl.

* * * * *

The next day, Juan Vásquez didn't come to work but he sent his kid. There was no way the boy could keep up by himself, and by law he couldn't go above the fifth rung on the ladder, where the red stripe was painted on the side of each leg. Gary,

the guy who drove the tractor and kept the crew lined out, ar-
ranged for the kid to work with the Salazars. Juan's ladder
stood by the tractor ruts as the crew pulled ahead, and when
the first trailer of the day filled up, Gary put the ladder on top
of the full bins and hauled it away.

That evening, I had a conversation with Juan Vásquez in
the bathroom. In his soft, smooth voice, he explained to me
that the peach fuzz had caused a terrible rash under his shirt.
He just couldn't take it. I didn't say anything, just nodded.

Jack Horton was a little more direct when I asked him
what he thought of it.

"Worthless son of a bitch. He's got the two girls workin',
and he sends the kid out on his own while he sits in the house
all day. I think he sneaks his drinks. Did you see how red his
eyes were? Peach fuzz, my ass."

"Actually, he was wearing sunglasses when I saw him."

"Sure he was. He'll wear 'em first thing in the mornin',
too, if he gets up that early."

"Like Al, huh?"

"Yeah, he's another one. Most peach farmers are out
there first daylight, before the crew, and they don't come in
till the last dog is hung."

I nodded in the direction of the neighbors' house. "You
think Juan drinks and hides it, then, huh?"

Jack took a pull from his bottle of Gallo. "Shit. He goes
to town every day and doesn't bring home any groceries. And
send those two girls out to work like that, and him sittin' on
his ass at home." He shook his head. "Could you imagine

Old Man Salazar pullin' that kind of shit? That's just the difference between people."

I had to admit that the Salazars—the old man and the boys at least—had it all over Juan Vásquez. They helped Bud and Cricket, and they let the Vásquez kid work on their set. They were the kind of family a fellow like Al Sagers liked to have working for him.

When I was back sitting on my own door sill, I saw a little flaw in the Salazars, the model fruit-picking family. The older of the two boys got out of the '59 Chevy, stretched, looked around, and then wandered down to the barn and around in back of it. Twenty minutes later, Cricket came out from the other side of the barn and walked to her house without looking aside once. A few minutes after that, the Salazar kid came back and sat in the front seat with his brother. I couldn't blame him. He was just taking what he could get, like most young guys would.

I couldn't blame her, either. Far from it. I felt sorry for her. She was trying hard to get the hell out of this kind of life, but she didn't know how to do it. And every time she tried, she had to go find someone else to make her feel better about how things went wrong. I didn't like to think about where she was headed, and I guessed there was some advantage to being a single guy and just having my own ass to look out for.

* * * * *

I've heard that a peach tree sweats a hundred gallons a day. I don't know if that's true, but I do know that a peach orchard

74

is a miserable place to be stuck in. The peach fuzz and the mosquitoes are bad enough, but the atmosphere is murder. Humidity comes up out of the ground where the orchard has been irrigated for the last couple of months, the trees hold the heat and moisture down, and the tall weeds hold it in on the sides. When Gary would haul us all out on the wagon at the end of the day, I would feel a big relief as we broke out into the thin, clear air. It didn't matter that the temperature was still a hundred degrees. Just feeling a little motion in the air made me feel like I'd gotten out of jail.

On the third morning after I had the quick in-and-out in the back seat of my car, Cricket and Bud didn't show up for work. The rest of us went on ahead, leaving their ladders standing by the drive. At about nine o'clock, when the sun was heating the orchard and the mosquitoes were in full swing, the two Salazar girls came running back screaming from where they had gone ahead to the edge of the orchard to tinkle.

At first I didn't pay them any attention, because they were always making noise about something, but as I went to the wagon with a bucket of peaches, I caught some of what they were saying to Gary.

"It looks like the girl who didn't come to work today. Just laying there."

Gary nodded and took the cigar out of his mouth. He was just a few years older than I was, not even thirty, I'd guess, but he smoked cigars to keep the mosquitoes away. He looked at me, at the sorter girls, and then at the two younger ones, who were still breathing hard as they stood there wide-eyed.

"I'll go take a look." He turned to me. "Charlie, how would you like to go with me?"

I felt the eyes of the two Vásquez girls on me. Lupe was barely a yard away on my left. "All right," I said as I stepped down from the running board. With my picking bucket still strapped on, I walked away from the wagon and joined Gary.

When we were several trees ahead of the pickers, he said, "You've got to be careful or you can lose the whole crew. Even something like a snake can do it. One person hollers out, and they're all gone."

I'd heard that about Mexicans, but I'd never seen it. To the contrary, I'd seen 'em all gather around when some guy had chopped the head off a bull snake. But I didn't say anything. I just walked along, thinking I could have left my bucket back at my ladder.

Since Gary had already pulled a couple of loads of peaches out this way, the clods in the drive were mashed. Gary walked in one track and I took the other. Here where the orchard hadn't been picked, the weeds grew up to meet the branches that hung down with the weight of the fruit. The place had a closed-in feeling.

"The girls said it was straight ahead and out toward the end of these two rows on the right." Gary waved his cigar.

A few trees from the end, we moved over to walk the next two rows. I was on the outside, next to where the orchard had been picked, where the weeds were trampled and the branches hung lighter. I usually didn't have much to do with a picked orchard, but whenever I had to go back to one, it had a tired look to it. That's the way it was now, as I walked between the part that was done with and the part that had a full crop.

We found Cricket in the weeds just inside the end of the orchard. She was lying face down, and the filtered sunlight coming through the Johnson grass was shining on her bleach-blond hair and pale legs. I didn't want to touch her, and I don't think Gary did either, but it was his part. He was the row boss.

He moved close enough to nudge her in the back with his field boot, and as he stepped back he said, "I'm pretty sure she's dead."

I felt it was my duty to look at her. She was lying with her left arm under her, her right arm flung out, and her legs splayed. Someone had just dumped her there, it looked like. "It's too bad," I said.

"Yeah, it sure is. I've got to hold this crew together."

I would have liked to have gotten way the hell away from there, but I knew it wouldn't do, so I just shrugged. "No reason for me to quit working."

He dropped his cigar and stepped on it. "Shit. This is going to be one big mess." He glanced at the body, shook his head, and turned away. "Let's go back."

* * * * *

The rest of the day was a big mess, just like he said. As soon as Gary was gone with a load of peaches, after leaving word that he was going to call Al and we should all keep working, the Salazars and the Vásquez kid walked out to the edge of the orchard by the road and sat there. The Hortons and I kept picking, but things went pretty slow at the wagon with less than half a crew. Chano gave his clipboard to Toni and went to see if he could talk the Salazars into coming back to work. I couldn't imagine the Vásquez girls being comfortable at all, knowing that the dead girl was out at the other end of the orchard, but they were getting paid by the hour, and they couldn't throw that away. As for myself, I didn't like the feeling at all either, but if Jack Horton could keep his kids at it, I thought I should do the same. And besides, at sixteen cents a bucket, it was the only way I was going to make anything.

At a little before noon, we heard hollering out by the road. It sounded like Gary and Chano taking turns, and one of the Vásquez girls said they were calling for us to come out. The Hortons and I slipped out of our picking harnesses and followed the girls in their wrapped-up, baggy outfits.

Al Sagers was there, having come from somewhere in his shiny new Malibu instead of the dusty GMC. Gary had come back with a wagonload of empty bins. And just pulling in on the other side of the boss's Malibu was a sheriff's car with two cops in it.

I stood at the edge and let everyone else talk. I knew enough Spanish to understand what Chano and Old Man Salazar were saying back and forth. The old man wanted to go home for the rest of the day. It was a hard thing to happen to his daughters. Chano explained that the boss wanted to fill out at least one truckload today, and he couldn't let all the fruit go to waste.

Gary asked Jack Horton what he thought.

Jack was squatted in the shade of a tree, smoking a Pall Mall. "Me 'n' my boys'll work. That's what we come for. We won't make a dime if we don't. But I don't think you can get these Mexicans to budge an inch until you get that girl out of there. Where the hell's Bud, anyway?"

Gary looked away for a second, then came back. "Um, he's in his cabin."

"Drunk?"

"I think that's why he didn't come to work today, but I don't know for sure what it has to do with the girl."

Jack raised his eyebrows. "You tell us when you want us to go back to work, and we'll do it. We're not making anything sittin' here."

One of the deputies, an older man with a lump on his left jaw, was standing back a step or two. Now he spoke. "We've got someone comin' to take away the body. Meanwhile, we'd like to keep everyone in the same place until we get a chance to talk to each one. Whoever wants to work in the meanwhile, that's fine." He turned to Gary. "But I'm gonna ask that you turn your crew around and work back this way so nothin' gets trampled out on that end where they found the body."

Gary hesitated. "It'll be a little trouble to have to go back and pick those trees, but we can do it. We'll finish the trees we're on, then move straight across and come back this way."

"I'd appreciate it."

Jack Horton spoke up. "Why the hell they dump that girl's body out here, do you think? Just so someone would find it?"

The deputy shook his head. "We don't know yet."

"Well, if that's why, they sure as hell got it done."

* * * * *

My turn for questioning came late in the afternoon. The last wagonload of the day was slow in filling up. The only ones left picking were the two Salazar boys, Jack Horton and his two sons, and me. Old Man Salazar had gone back to camp with his two girls, and the Vásquez kid had seen the chance to go along. County vehicles had been coming and going in the part of the orchard we had left behind, and the whole place seemed out of whack. When Gary told me it was my turn, he said, "I hope it doesn't take long. That truck's been waitin' all day."

I left my bucket on the bottom step of my ladder and walked out to the edge of the orchard. The two cops were the only people there. The one with the lump on his jaw did the questioning while the younger one, a fellow in slick dark hair, wrote down the notes. I saw the older one's brass tag with the name of Wagstaff.

"You're Charlie?"

"That's right. Charlie Mullen."

"How old are you, Charlie?"

"Twenty-five."

"And you've been on this crew for about a week?"

"A little less."

"Long enough to know the deceased, though."

I shrugged. "A little."

"How much?"

"Not much. Just a little. Work in the same field, live in the same camp."

"Uh-huh. Did you ever leave camp with her?"

A little warning went up in my mind. Don't lie to the cops, especially if it's something you can get caught up on. "Once," I answered. "Three nights ago."

"Where did you go?"

"To a canal bank. Not for very long."

The cop looked me over in a way I didn't like. Other cops had done it before. It was like an appraisal of some lower form of life. "You know you can get in trouble with girls that age."

I pushed the edge of truth this time. "She gave me to understand she was of age."

"I bet." Then, as if he was correcting his tone, he asked. "Did you know she was pregnant?"

"She didn't mention it, but I might have seen something that looked like that."

"You mean she was starting to show."

"I didn't notice it until we were out on the canal bank."

"You mean when she had her clothes off."

"Well, yeah."

He let out a heavy breath. "What did you two talk about?"

"Not much, really. She seemed to be lookin' for someone to run off with."

"I see. She suggested that to you?"

"Yes, she did."

"And you didn't take her up on it?"

"No, I didn't."

"And what did she say to that?"

"Oh, about what you'd expect. She kind of flew off the handle, sayin' how we were all the same, just after one thing."

His eyebrows went up and down. "Did you do anything to try to quiet her down, like slap her or shake her?"

I drew back. "No, not at all. She calmed down by herself."

"What about last night?"

"What about it?"

"Did you take her out last night?"

"Oh, no. She was done with me the first time. She didn't as much as look at me after that."

"Where were you last night?"

"In my tent."

"All night?"

"Yeah. I went to bed when it was gettin' dark, and I didn't get up until I heard everyone stirrin' around camp this morning."

"Did anyone see you?"

"You mean sleeping in my tent? They would have had to peek in with a flashlight. Why?"

"Well, the other boy that was pokin' her was with the rest of his family. They can vouch for him."

I got a little burned at that point. "Well," I said, "I don't have any witnesses to say I didn't do anything, but you sure as hell won't find anyone who can say I did, because I didn't leave my tent."

"Sure," he said, not very apologetic. "I've just got to ask." He looked at the other cop. "Anything else?" The younger cop shook his head.

"Can I go back to work?"

"I suppose so. But I'd recommend you not leave this county for a few days at least."

"This is only my fifth day of work."

He gave me the appraising look again. "Some people don't last that long."

* * * * *

The camp was full of hubbub that evening. Juan Vásquez was down at the Salazar house, talking to the old man on the front step as the two boys listened on. The sound of a radio came out of Bud's front door, but the man stayed inside. I went to visit Jack Horton to see what he thought about all of it.

"That lazy-ass next door is tryin' to get a strike goin'. He came over here, and I told him I wasn't goin' to have anything to do with it, so he went down to Salazar's."

"Yeah, he's been talkin' to him for an hour. What's his idea?"

"Just a bunch of shit, that's what. Says he's lookin' out for his daughters. I think he sees where the boss is worried about gettin' behind, and he wants to get the others to do a sit-down for a day."

"What's he stand to get out of that? Those girls'll just lose a day's wages, or more."

"I 'magine he wants to get 'em a raise, another dime an hour, and he sees this as his chance."

"That's unbelievable," I said.

"Yeah, as if he gave a damn about the safety of the girls. He sends 'em out on their own to bring in the money. I don't think he cares about anything else."

"Like the poor girl that got killed."

"Yeah, and him tryin' to get somethin' for himself out of it. There's no good in that."

"Does anyone know how she got killed?"

"Got knocked in the head is what I heard."

I winced. "Have you talked to Bud?"

"He's drunk off his ass."

"Does anyone think he did it?"

"Nah. He was up late drinkin', waitin' for the girl to come in. Neighbors noticed it 'cause it kept some of them awake, the lights on."

I thought of Cricket as I saw her that last time, lying in the weeds. "Well, it's too bad."

"No good in any of it. Best thing we can do is just go to work in the mornin', mind our own business."

As I was on my way back to my tent, I saw Juan Vásquez stop at Bud's door. I sat in my doorway to watch what might come of that.

I heard their voices play back and forth. I couldn't pick up any words, but the tone started rising. It went on for several minutes until the screen door creaked open and banged shut, and Bud came out hollering. A few seconds later, he and Juan were punching each other and cussing. Then Juan knocked him down, knelt over, and kept swinging. I jumped up and ran across the way to try to keep Juan from going too far. I looked to make sure he wasn't holding a knife or anything, and then I tackled him.

We all three got up and stood apart from one another.

Juan spoke first. "What you knock me down for?"

"He's drunk. You don't need to hurt him anymore."

"He better watch his mouth, that's all I say."

I looked at Bud, who was on his feet but weaving. "Are you all right?" I said.

People were starting to gather around—the Salazar boys, Chano, Juan's son and two daughters. Even Jack Horton had come out and was standing close enough to listen.

Bud's voice was slurred. "You're just a dirty Mexican. Good for nothin'. Chances are, you did it."

"I tell you, Bud. You better watch your mouth."

I thought Bud was going to fall down as he looked around and shifted his feet, but he stayed up.

"None of you gives a damn," he said, "but I'll tell you, someone's gonna pay for it." He stared at the Salazar kid and then at Juan. "Someone."

Juan held his chin up. "You better look somewhere else, Bud. I didn't have nothin' to do with your daughter. I'm sorry what happened to her, but I can't let you say that kinda shit." He turned and walked toward his house.

I took a couple of steps in Bud's direction. "Do you need any help gettin' back into your house?"

"Piss on you," he slurred. "You're as bad as the rest of 'em." He staggered to his house and went inside.

All the others had pretty much drifted back to their own places, but I didn't go to my tent. For as much as I didn't like him, I felt I owed Juan Vásquez an apology, and even at that I don't think I would have gone to his house if it hadn't been for his daughters. Dusk was falling, and as I walked toward his front door, I saw one of the two girls sitting on a chair on the other side of the step.

Rather than knock on the door, I stopped a few feet away. From the shape of her face, I could tell it was Lupe. She had her hair let down, and it looked as if she had washed it earlier. It covered her shoulders.

"I'm sorry for anything I did to your dad."

"Oh, that's all right."

"He probably thought I was gangin' up on him, but I just wanted to break things up."

"Don't worry. That other man was pretty drunk."

"If I'd known what he said, or what he was going to say, I might not have bothered."

"It doesn't matter. It's all over now."

"Well, tell your dad I'm sorry, if you will. I don't want him to think I'm takin' sides."

"It's all right. I'll tell him."

* * * * *

Most of the crew was back on the job the next day. Juan, of course, stayed in camp, and so did Bud. His ladder and Cricket's stood where they had been the day before. The rest of us worked like ants, crawling through the orchard and stripping the trees. Chano whistled and sang, but no one else had much to say. I didn't hear anything more about a strike.

That evening, the deputies came into camp and asked another round of questions. Like before, they came to me last. They didn't ask me anything new, but they pressed me on the subject of where I was when Cricket disappeared and why I couldn't think of anyone who had seen me go to bed early. I could tell they had me on their list of suspects, and I didn't care for the way the lumpy-jawed one, Wagstaff, ended the conversation.

"Don't think about goin' anywhere," he said. "I've told your boss to let us know if you ask for a draw of any kind."

"Don't worry," I said. "I've got nothing to run from."

* * * * *

Four more pickers showed up the next day, all of them in a station wagon with Oregon plates. It looked like a man, his wife, their daughter, and her husband. They were all lean and light-haired, and in spite of their license plates, they sounded like they were from Oklahoma or Texas. They took Bud and Cricket's ladders, and Gary brought them two more. They didn't talk much to anyone else, so the crew stayed pretty quiet. I doubt that anyone told them about the big event a few days before, as they didn't seem to be curious about anything. That evening they moved into two of the empty tent cabins.

I guessed everyone but Bud would like to see the whole thing blow over, but I didn't like being under suspicion, and I wished I could find someone who could at least speak for me having been in my tent. The cops gave me the impression they had already quizzed everyone about me, and I didn't want to make things worse by going around and asking for an alibi. But I wished I could sound someone out, so when I saw Lupe Vásquez sitting by her doorstep that evening, I stopped and said hello. When she said hello in return, I thought I might get a conversation started.

"It looks like we've got more of a crew going now."

"I guess so."

"As soon as we finish this orchard, he's got another one ready. That's what Gary says."

"Yeah."

Silence hung for a second until I said, "How long do you think the season will last?"

"I don't know."

"Well, everyone wants to make as much as they can."

"Sure."

"Maybe it's all the same to you."

"How is that?" Her voice sounded defensive.

"Oh, well, I mean, you and your sister work by the hour. You don't have a good day or a bad day."

"I guess."

"And the boss seems to treat you well."

She let out an impatient breath. "Oh, him."

"Don't you like him? I thought you did."

"Why?"

"Well, he put you on sorting. That's better than picking. It's a step up, anyway, even if you don't make any more."

"I hate all of it."

"I don't blame you for that. But at least the boss gave you a little better job."

"You make him sound so generous."

"Well."

"He's like everyone else. He wants something."

I felt criticized myself. "Girls always say that, too. Sometimes they're right, but not everyone's always that way."

"Well, this one is."

"You mean because of the way he acts, like a big shot?"

"No, because of what he said."

"Really? He just came right out and said it?"

"He told me I could be riding around in a nice car."

I felt a funny shiver as I heard those words. "Huh. I guess he does have a nice car, as far as that's concerned."

"Lots of guys do. And younger ones than him. But that doesn't mean just any girl is going to go with them, just for that."

"I would guess some do, or the guys wouldn't try it."

She folded her arms across her front. "Maybe some do, but I don't."

I didn't have an answer for that. I was caught halfway between admiring her for her pride and feeling sorry for her for being so cold and bitter. In addition to that, I was picturing Al Sagers's shiny Malibu.

* * * * *

We had worked through Sunday like any other day, trying to

get caught up, and when we finished the orchard we were in, it was about two in the afternoon on a Wednesday. Gary said we could start the next field in the morning, and he asked me if I would like to work another hour with him and Chano, moving the ladders. I said sure, with nothing else to do any-way, so we loaded everything up on an empty wagon. With Chano on one side and me on the other, keeping the ladders from spilling off, we rattled along the side of the road for half a mile till we came to the next orchard.

When we got the ladders unloaded and all standing up, Gary said he had to go back and get another tractor so he could disk the drives. At about that time, Al Sagers showed up in his GMC and said he had another hour's work for me if I wanted it. I asked what it was, and he said he wanted to flag some trees at the other end. I said okay, and I got into the cab with him as Gary and Chano pulled away.

"What are we gonna flag the trees for?" I asked.

"We were supposed to knock the last two rows as part of the green drop, but it didn't get done. I need to go through and flag 'em all so they don't get picked."

"Does all that fruit go to waste?"

"It's got to. It should've been done earlier. Now it's all got to be knocked and disked in, or I'll have brown rot till hell won't have it."

He cocked his head back and looked straight ahead, and his dark glasses seemed like a shield. I got the impression that I wasn't important enough for him to talk to any more than he had to, so I lit a cigarette and kept to myself as he shifted gears and drove to the end of the orchard. I glanced around the cab

90

of the pickup, and it looked normal—a pack of Marlboros on the dashboard, a two-way radio, the gearshift sticking up through a pile of rings for sizing peaches, a roll of blue plastic ribbon on the seat between us.

He let me out at the corner of the field. The rows were uneven at this end because the orchard ran along the river. Al told me to tie a streamer of ribbon on the west side of each of the last two trees of every row.

"I'll pick you up at the other corner in about an hour," he said. Then he turned the pickup around and drove back the way we came.

From where I stood, I could smell the river but I couldn't quite see it. A jungle of oak trees, elderberry bushes, and wild grapevines grew along the edge, and the weeds were dry there. In the orchard, where it had been irrigated up until a few days before, the weeds grew tall and green. The air was heavy, hot and humid, and the mosquitoes whined in my ears. I worked as fast as I could, tagging all the trees like he told me, and all the time wondering why no one from the peach advisory board had come out to verify the green drop. This was the first time I'd heard of someone getting away with something like this, but if he was flagging the trees, it was for a reason.

When I got to the other corner, he was sitting in the pickup, smoking a cigarette. His farmer's cap was set back on his head, but he had his dark glasses in place. The window on my side was still rolled down, and when I went to open the door, he said, "There's another little thing I want to look at here." He got out of the cab and said, across the bed in back, "Get that shovel there."

I reached in and pulled out an irrigator's shovel that sat on top of a jumble of rubber boots and aluminum siphon tubes. He lifted a pick out of his side and said, "Over here."

I followed him out past the edge of the orchard where the tractors turned around, then down a slope toward the river. The oak trees and jungle were about fifty yards away at this spot, and I could see the water through the branches. Where I was following the boss, it was mostly bull thistle and pigweed, dry and drying. Down the slope, we came to a level area.

"There's a pipeline under here somewhere," he said. "As soon as we get this orchard picked, I have to get it dug up. I need to know where it is."

"Does it drain into the river or pull water out?"

"Pulls it out, but it's not workin' worth a shit. Here. Start with the shovel, and if it gets hard goin', I'll spell you with the pick."

The dirt was loose, sandy stuff, even a little damp, and the digging went easy. I started with a hole about two feet square, and after I got down about a foot and a half, he said, "Dig it out a little more on each side."

That was all right, as it gave me more room to work in.

"Do you need the pick?" he asked.

"No, it's not all that dry. Does the run-off from the orchard come here?"

"Some of it, I think."

I kept digging, and he stood a few feet back, fidgeting around with the pick. He'd stand it with the head up, bang the handle on the ground, and loosen the head. Then he'd turn it around and tamp the other end of the handle on the ground, as if he wanted to snug the head back onto the thick end.

Once I looked up at him to see what the hell he was doing, and he said, "You need to dig some more this way."

I carved at the side until I had a hole about four by three and more than two feet deep, and I was ready for a break. "Do we have any water?" I asked.

"Sure. Climb on out of there."

I set the shovel lengthwise along the edge of the hole and was pushing myself up on it when I saw that he had gotten the pick head off the handle and was coming down on me with that thick piece of wood, like a baseball bat. I pushed backward, and as he swung past me he lost balance and fell into the pit with me.

It was a real fight then, all dirt and sweat and short, off-center punches. He was bigger than I was, and he wrestled to get his arm around my throat. I felt it crush my Adam's apple, and then I thrashed and squirmed until I broke loose. I scrambled out of the pit, and he came right after me.

All I could think of was that this guy wanted to kill me and I couldn't let him do it. He had the pick handle in his right hand now, and I yanked the shovel off the ground and brought it around with both hands so I could swing it. He passed the pick handle to his left hand, bent to the pile of loose dirt I had dug out, and grabbed a handful with his right hand. His dark glasses had fallen off, and I could see his bloodshot eyes searching for an open spot.

"You piece of trash," he said. He faked a jab with the pick handle, then threw the dirt at my face, grabbed his club with both hands, and moved in.

I got dirt in my face, but I swung the shovel with all I had. He tried to bring his stick up to block me, but I knocked it aside and glanced the flat of the shovel head against his ear. He staggered but didn't go down, so I whacked him again, a little squarer this time. He went down.

I stood back, leaning on the shovel. I was taking huge, deep breaths. All I could think of, still, was that this son of a bitch wanted to kill me.

Then I let things come back to me. I was out on the edge of an orchard, and this guy had played me for a fool. Blue ribbons, green drop, a pipe to dig up. If there was a pipeline drawing water from the river, there should be a pump nearby. All I was doing was digging a hole, and once this guy had me in it, he could get rid of my car, tell the cops he gave me a draw, and make it look like I skipped out.

I had to get to the cops first, whether he was alive or not. I crouched near him and watched. I didn't want to touch him to feel for a pulse, but I wanted to see if he moved at all. After a minute I could see he was breathing, so I got up and moved fast.

The easiest way would be to go in his pickup, but I wasn't going to leave myself open to any accusations there. I pulled the keys from the ignition, yanked the head off the two-way radio, and took off on foot through the orchard.

When I came out by the road, I stopped long enough to take a few deep breaths in the open air. Then I hoofed it to the labor camp.

I was dirty, sweaty, thirsty, sore, and washed out when I got there, but I knew I had no time to lose. The camp, on the other hand, was quiet and calm. The only car that was gone was Jack Horton's, and I figured he had gone to the liquor store. Lupe Vásquez came to the doorway to look at me and then went back inside. Chano came out of the bathroom, clean and shiny, and waved as he walked to his tent.

I got a drink of water inside my own tent and then stood by the front door of my car, wondering if I should leave in it. I knew there wasn't a telephone in the labor camp, and my best bet would be to drive into town to the sheriff's office. I wished to hell I had a friend to go with me, to vouch that I wasn't running away.

After a few minutes of standing in the sun I decided to go in my car, and I no sooner had it started up than a sheriff's car pulled in with the same two cops as always. I shut off the engine and got out. The cop car pulled up next to me with the window rolled down, and the one who always did the questioning, Wagstaff, was driving. I handed him the keys to the GMC.

"What's this? Are you turning yourself in?"

"I think I know where your man is."

"What man?"

"The one who knocked up Cricket and tried to keep her quiet."

"The hell. Where is he, then?"

"Out at the end of the orchard, where he tried to finish me off with a pick handle. Those are his keys."

Wagstaff looked me over. "You're dirty enough." He turned to the other deputy. "Go ahead and search him, and let him get in back. We'll go take a look."

That's cops for you. When I was in the back seat and the car was pulling around, I saw Lupe Vásquez come to the door again. I figured she thought I was getting hauled away. Maybe she felt sorry for me, and maybe she didn't care. Either way was all right. I was more like her than either of us had realized. Even if I was just a fruit tramp, and even if she knew I had screwed Cricket in the back seat of my car, I had my pride, and I'd be back to get my stuff before I left.

Born to Lose

As I drove down the last stretch of gravel road to the ranch and turned into the parking area, I saw a few men gathered around the back of Benny's pickup. I parked my car next to the others, where it would be in the shade of the sycamore trees for the first half of the day, and I shut off the engine. Ed and I got out and wandered over toward the group of men.

The hubbub was coming to an end. Laketree, the ranch superintendent, was talking in a high, cheery tone. "That's great, just great. I'll call and have someone come out and get it."

His face was beaming as he turned away from the little crowd. He and Vic the bookkeeper walked into the main office, and Pat the mechanic ambled back to the shop. Only Benny and the guy who worked with him, Miguel, were left, and they stood aside to let us see what they had.

Benny's pickup was a tan Ford, about 1960, with an aluminum camper shell on back. The tailgate was down and the flap of the camper was up, but the interior was shady. It took me a second to see the deer lying on its back with its legs up and spread out.

Benny didn't look at us. He kept his eye on the animal as he said, "It's a doe. I killed it."

Miguel said something in Spanish, and Benny nodded.

I didn't think it was hunting season yet. "Are you going to eat it?" I asked.

"No, they gonna take it to the county jail."

Miguel nodded and said, "*Ah, sí.*"

Benny raised his head as if he was looking at a trophy. He was taller than most Mexicans, with broad shoulders. He always wore khakis and a tan jungle helmet to match. He had narrow eyes and a clipped mustache. Today he had a little stubble on his chin, and his eyes had a tinge of pink. From that, and the swelling of the deer's belly, and the stiffness of its legs, I imagined he had gotten to the ranch pretty early.

There didn't seem to be anything else to say. Benny and Miguel worked under Frank in the prune orchards, while Ed and I worked for Clarence in the walnuts, and this was the first time I had even exchanged words with Frank's men. I turned to walk away, and Ed went with me. He hadn't said a word, and I don't think he liked Mexicans.

Clarence came out of the shop with a shovel in his hand. It looked as if he had been grinding an edge on it. "You and Ed can go ahead and do as you've been doin'," he said.

I tossed my head toward the main office. "Looks like Benny killed a deer."

"Yeah. That's how he makes points with the big boss." Clarence gave a frown. "Doe like that, what's she going to do? Eat the green prunes? I wouldn't kill 'em like that even if I had bean fields. At least they eat the bean vines. I know that."

"Do they get a license to kill 'em out of season?"

"Oh, sure. Anti-depredation permit. That's big business for you."

I recalled the expression on Laketree's face. That was it. Run this outfit like the corporation that it was. Then there was Benny, who must have done it for the pleasure of killing the deer and kissing up to the big boss.

"Benny must have gotten here early," I said.

"Oh, yeah. Does it on his own time, with his own pickup and .22—and spotlight, I'd guess."

I waited a few seconds and said, "I've never hunted."

"Well, I have. And that's not huntin'."

Ed and I got our lunch pails and water, then climbed into the Chevy pickup we used. All the old pickups like ours were grey, and the ones that weren't quite so old were light green. I gunned the engine, let it run for a couple of minutes, and ground the floor shift into reverse. I backed out onto the gravel, turned, and swung around forward. Benny and Miguel were sitting in the cab of the tan Ford, in front of the office building with the sign on the wall that read "Make Accident Prevention a Part of Every Job."

* * * * *

Ed and I pulled hoses and set sprinklers until noon. We worked in fields 56 and 57, where the young walnut trees were tied to wooden stakes. Ed wasn't very good at finding the sprinklers in the tall weeds at the end of the field, and that was where the high-school kids running the mowers chopped up most of the hoses and sprinklers that they got. They took out stakes just about anywhere. Ed and I kept track of how many sprinklers needed to be fixed and how many stakes had to be replaced, and about every three days we did repairs.

Today was one of those days. After lunch, we got the glue and the couplings and the coil of hose out of the pickup. We started with a mangled hose at the edge of field 56. Ed was quite a talker when we worked close together, and he went on about how he and Chet went down to Sac in Chet's Cad. I had met Chet one time. He was a tall, raw-boned, sunburned ga-loot with a heavy brow and deep eyes. I think he was pretty awkward around people, so he and Ed, who didn't have a car or any other friends I knew of, made a pretty good pair. Ac-cording to Ed, they drove to Sac at a hundred miles an hour and picked up girls at drive-in hamburger joints. I listened to his stories and thought, yeah-yeah. I believed the part about how fast they drove.

Then he went on about an all-night café he went to, right there in town, and a waitress who he said kind of liked him. We were both standing up at that moment, and he looked straight at me with a confidential look on his face. He squinted his eyes a little and nodded his head. "Of course, she's married, so I can't do anything about it."

For the next couple of days as we drove back and forth from work, Ed mentioned the waitress from time to time. Her name was Claudette. She worked in the restaurant five nights a week and dealt cards the other two. Her husband was on disability for a bad back. She was three years older than Ed was, but age didn't make a difference. If she didn't have that husband, he might do something.

I couldn't imagine Ed making much of a move on anyone. He was twenty-two years old and still lived with his parents. From what I gathered, he never lasted at a job more than a month or so. A couple of times when I dropped him off I saw his sister, who was a year younger than he was and terribly ugly. She had scraggly hair, bad teeth, a dumpy build, and a loud voice to make things worse. I wondered if his angel Claudette looked any better.

* * * * *

On Friday night, after I cashed my paycheck and got cleaned up, I went to the restaurant where he said she worked. It was called the Wagon Wheel.

There were two waitresses on duty—an old, wrinkled woman about sixty and a heavy-set woman about forty. I drew the heavy-set one, and as she took my order I saw the name Shirley on her tag. I had the roast beef dinner, followed by apple pie. I took my time with a cup of coffee after that.

At about eight, the crowd thinned out and the two dinner waitresses finished their shift. The older one sat down at a booth to smoke a cigarette and count her tips, while Shirley slung her purse over her shoulder and went out the front door. Then I saw another waitress between the counter and the kitchen. I hadn't seen her come in, but she was already at work making a pot of coffee.

She wore a white blouse and a black skirt like the other two, and she had her back to me, so I looked at her for a few seconds. She had reddish-blond hair, which I was sure she dyed, and a nice figure that her waitress outfit didn't hide. She looked familiar to me.

Then, as if he was coming on shift, too, Ed walked through the front door. He headed for the counter and gave the waitress a wave. He was all slicked up and wearing a lightweight, black leather jacket, which I thought was a little much on a warm summer night.

He glanced around, saw me, and turned. A smile spread across his face. "Look who's here," he said. He had on his squinty look and bobbed his head back and forth.

"Sit down if you'd like. I just had dinner, and I'm havin' a cup of coffee. Care for some?"

"It's my middle name." He pulled out a chair and took a seat. He was clean-shaven, but he had a rough complexion, and I could see where he had nicked himself.

The waitress came right over with pretty good motion, carrying a glass coffee pot. She picked a cup off of the next table and set it in front of Ed.

"Hi, Claudette."

"Hi, Ed. You care for anything else, or just coffee?"

He had kind of a moon face when he smiled. "This'll be fine."

She looked at me.

"Put his on my tab," I said. "But I'm in no hurry to go."

"Sure." She topped off my cup and turned away.

As I watched her walk to the kitchen, I realized where I knew her from. She and her husband stayed at the Travelers Court, where I did.

"What's new, Ed?"

"Not much. Just killin' time."

"I thought maybe you would have gone to Sac."

His smile narrowed his eyes as he moved his head up and down. "Maybe tomorrow."

I thought we might have already run out of things to talk about. As I tried to think of another subject, Ed looked over at Claudette and motioned with his hand. As she came our way, he reached into his jacket pocket and brought out a quarter.

She seemed to know what to expect as she stood near him and waited.

"Here," he said. "Why don't you play J-4, and then something for yourself?"

"And the third one?"

He shrugged. "You can pick that one, too." He raised his head and took a drink of his coffee as she walked away.

I watched her. I heard the clunk of the quarter as she dropped it into the jukebox, and a few seconds later, a slow song came on. Then I recognized Ray Charles's voice as he sang "Born to Lose."

Ed had his eyes half-closed and was rocking his head back and forth. I guessed that he played the song every time he came in, so I didn't say anything as the sad voice went on.

The tempo changed with the next song as Ray Price sang "Crazy Arms," but there still didn't seem to be much to say. I looked around at the varnished pine walls, and my gaze settled on a mounted deer head with a big set of antlers. Beneath it was a little plaque with three lines that read *Jay Johnson. Modoc. 1957.* I glanced at Claudette, who had lit a cigarette and was blowing the smoke at the ceiling.

I had the feeling I was stuck back in time until the third song came on. I was expecting something like "Pearly Shells," but here came Creedence Clearwater Revival with "Bad Moon Rising," right off the charts. Claudette was tapping her fingers on the counter top, and Ed was rocking his head back and forth.

When the third song ended, I said, "I think I'm goin' to take off, Ed. Thanks for the company."

"Sure," he said. "Thanks for the coffee."

When I stood up, he did. "Can I give you a ride?" I asked.

"Oh, no. I think I'll sit at the counter for a while."

I left two quarters for a tip and headed for the cash register. Claudette set the ticket on the counter top and rang up my bill. As I handed her a five and waited for change, I saw Ed at the edge of my vision. He had moved to the jukebox and was feeding in a quarter.

I thanked Claudette, she thanked me, and I crossed paths with Ed as I went for the door. "Good night, Ed."

"G'night."

As I walked across the wood floor, I heard Ray Charles again with the smooth, sad words of "Born to Lose."

* * * * *

I was sitting outside my room at the Travelers Court on a warm weekday evening when Claudette's husband came by.

He was wearing a pale green T-shirt and a pair of blue jeans. He had light brown hair combed up and over like James Dean. If he had a collar he would have had it turned up. He had a lit cigarette in his hand and a pack in his shirt pocket.

"Hey," he said. "You've got the right idea, sittin' outside where it's a little cooler."

I shrugged. "When it gets hot it stays that way."

"Isn't that the truth." He took a drag on his cigarette. "Say, my battery's dead, and I wonder if I can get a ride to the store."

"I guess I could. Let me get my keys." I went inside for my keys and wallet, and he was looking up at the power lines when I came out. "Go ahead and get in," I said. "It's un-locked." He got in as I went around to my door. I settled in behind the wheel and put the key in the ignition. "Which store do you want to go to?"

"Over here to the Westside."

"Oh." I realized he meant the Westside Liquor. I backed up, then pulled out onto the street.

He rolled down the window and flicked his ashes. "I'll be happy to give you a beer for your trouble."

"Nah, that's okay. I don't want to drink up your supply."

"It's a small deal. As far as that's concerned, if you wanted to, we could go in together on a six-pack." He smiled. "That way I wouldn't drink so much."

I felt stuck. He had offered me a beer, and now I felt like I'd be a moocher if I didn't help pay.

"Here," he said. "I've got five quarters. If you've got three, we can a get a six-pack of Lucky."

"All I've got is dollar bills."

"Well, that's fine. You give me a dollar, and you keep a quarter. That's the least I can do."

I drove another block and pulled into the Westside. It wasn't that far to begin with. I took out a dollar and gave it to him.

"Here." He handed me a quarter.

"Nah, you keep it."

"I wouldn't feel right if I did. I'm serious." He laid the quarter on the seat between us and got out. A couple of minutes later he came back with a brown bag. He pushed the quarter toward me as he got in.

I gave up and took the quarter. As I put it in my pocket, I wondered if it was one of the two I left his wife. I assumed when he had five quarters to begin with that he was spending her tips.

Back at the court he said, "Why don't I go get a chair? If you don't mind, we can sit outside your place and drink these."

"That's fine."

He went and got the chair that was outside their room, and when he came back I handed him a can of Lucky Lager.

"I put the other four in the refrigerator."

"Good. I would have mentioned it if you didn't." He sat down, popped his beer, and took a drink. Then he let out a breath and said, "Ahhh, that's good."

"Sure is."

He settled into his chair and lit a cigarette. "By the way, my name's Woody. Woody Hudspeth."

"I'm Russ Nolan."

"Wife says she knows you."

"Just barely. I ate dinner there last Friday. Fellow I work with, I think he goes in there for coffee."

"Which fella is that?"

"Name of Ed."

"Oh, uh-huh."

I thought maybe he was going to ask me about Ed, but he surprised me.

"That Mexican named Benny works with you too, doesn't he?"

"Well, he works on the same ranch, but we're under different foremen."

"What do you think of him?"

"Benny? Oh, I hardly know him."

"Thinks he's King Shit, doesn't he?"

"I don't know. Maybe he lords it over some of the other Mexicans. How do you know him?"

"He hangs around the card room where she works. I go in there once in a while myself, and he usually comes through about midnight, all scrubbed up and smellin' like a French whore."

I'd like to have a dollar for every guy I've heard use that expression, and I doubt that a single one of them ever smelled a real French whore in person. "I didn't know he stayed up that late," I said.

"He's a smooth one. He goes straight home from work and sleeps a few hours. Then he gets pimped up and cruises through the bars and card rooms. He goes home when the bars close, unless he's got somethin' to do, and he sleeps another three hours until he gets up for work."

"Unless he's got somethin' to do—?"

"I guess he screwin' the other card dealer. They say he's got a big dick."

"Sounds like they know everything about him."

"He's got a wife and kids at home. And here he is, sleepin' a split shift and out trollin' with his dick at all hours of the night." Woody tipped up his beer and drained it. "Boy, that one went fast. You ready for another?"

"Not yet, but I'll get you one."

He stayed ahead of me and drank four to my two. He brought up the subject of Benny again, but when he didn't get much out of me he dropped it. He talked about fishing, but I didn't have much to say on that, either. When we killed off the six-pack, I yawned and said I needed to turn in.

Woody stood up and said, "You bet. We'll get together again and shoot the shit. I like you."

* * * * *

For the next few days, as I pulled out hoses and set sprinklers, and as I listened to Ed's chatter about meeting girls in Chet's Cad, I couldn't help thinking about Benny. I wondered if he led the double life Woody said he did, or whether the reputation was bigger than the man, so to speak, and whether Woody was just afraid that Benny was going to screw his wife. Or maybe he was already doing it.

I wondered about it even more when I saw Claudette coming and going, which wasn't very often. Then one evening when my door was open and I was sitting inside reading the want ads, she knocked on the door frame.

"Can you give me a ride?" she said. "This battery has run down again, and I've got clothes at the laundromat."

It was dark outside, and I was about ready to go to bed, but I took a deep breath and said, "Okay."

When we got into the car, I could smell fried food. She was in her white blouse and black skirt. "Don't you usually work the night shift?" I asked.

"Yeah, but I switched with another gal. I did the dinner shift, and I thought I would get some laundry done. But then the battery goes dead again, and he's passed out asleep."

I thought I caught something in her tone, but I looked straight ahead as I drove to the laundromat. Her clothes were done, so I watched as she put everything in two cardboard boxes, and then I helped her carry them out to the car.

Back at Travelers Court, I parked in my regular spot and helped her unload her clean laundry.

"I really appreciate this," she said as she came back for the second box. "I'll check and see if there's any beer in the fridge, and if there is, I'll bring you one."

"Oh, you don't have to."

"No, but you didn't have to give me a ride, either. So it's the least I can do."

I went into my room and wondered what I could expect. A couple of minutes later, I heard a knock on the door. Claudette stood there holding two cans of Lucky.

"Come on in," I said. I held the door open, then closed it when she walked through. "We can sit here." We each took a chair at the little table that sat in the path of the window fan.

She pushed a beer toward me, popped hers open, and blew upwards at her bangs. "Jesus. It's just one thing after another."

"You need to take it easy." It sounded dumb as I said it, as far as the words went, but I thought it was the way she wanted to be talked to. I took a drink of my beer and smiled at her.

She reached up and touched her hair. "I must look terrible."

"No, you look fine."

She took a sip of beer. "I don't drink much of this stuff."

"A little won't hurt you."

She touched her hair again. "I feel like everything's out of place. Do you have a mirror?"

"Sure. It's in the bathroom." I stood up and motioned with my arm.

She rose from her chair and passed close by me. She clicked on the bathroom light and left the door open as she dabbed at her hair. Then she switched off the light and headed back.

On a hunch I picked up her beer and had it ready for her as she came near me.

She stopped about two feet away and took the can. "Why, thank you." She stood not quite facing me, and her eyes brushed over me as she took a sip of beer.

I took a drink of mine and smiled. "Relaxing?"

"A little."

I shrugged. "Well, this is all right."

"Sure." She tightened her brows, as if she was deciding something.

"I think your hair looks fine."

"It's nice of you to say that, but I just saw myself."

"No, I mean it. You look fine."

Her glance slid over me.

"I mean it."

Her eyes flickered, and I think she was done deciding. She said, "I should probably be going."

"Oh, don't be in a hurry."

"I'm not. I just need to go." She stepped aside and set her beer on the table.

I felt my spirits sinking, but I didn't have a right to anything, so I said, "Well, feel free to drop by again some time."

"Sure. And thanks again for helping me with my laundry."

"Thanks for the beer."

"You bet."

As I watched her walk out, I thought there had been a moment when it might have been possible and then the moment passed. It made me feel a little jealous, because I was sure she had decided and didn't make the same decision as she might in some other case. I didn't let it bother me too much, though. I finished my beer, poured hers down the drain, and went to bed.

* * * * *

Prune harvest started a few days later, and when Ed and I got to work we saw Benny driving a tractor with a shaker boom mounted on it. He was wearing a yellow hard hat, and for a moment I imagined that the boom was a battering ram and Benny was setting out on a combat mission at five miles an hour.

"See there, Ed? You stick with it, and you could be some foreman's right-hand man."

"That's shit. I'd rather go back to washin' dishes than be like him."

"Washin' dishes might not be all that bad, dependin' on who you get to work with."

"I'm not in a mood for any of that right now," he said.

It was as if a little light went on. I would have bet money that Ed had either found out or figured out that Benny was screwing his angel Claudette.

* * * * *

Things took an interesting turn the next day when we got to work and saw Claudette's husband, Woody, standing outside the main office smoking a cigarette.

Ed went up and asked him what he was doing there.

"Workin'. I'm gonna be runnin' the scales, weighin' the trailer loads of prunes as they come in." He glanced at me. "Hey," he said.

I realized I had seen his car in the parking lot when I left the auto court that morning, and he had gotten to work ahead of us. "How'd you get here?" I asked.

"I rode with Benny."

I heard Ed take in a quick breath, and when I looked at him I thought he was fit to chew nails. "We'd better get goin'," I said.

Woody dropped his cigarette and stepped on it. "Take it easy."

As I warmed up the old grey Chevy, Ed went into the shop. I figured he was going to talk to Pat the mechanic. When he came out, he climbed into the cab and slammed the door. His eyes were narrower than usual, and I thought smoke would come out of his ears.

"This is real shit," he said.

"What is?"

"Pat said Benny finagled that guy a job."

"Not too bad a one. Gets to sit on his ass all day and weigh a load once or twice an hour."

"His disability ran out, and he gets Benny to get him a job. If he knew what kind of a—"

"Maybe he does."

"Oh, my God." Ed stomped his foot on the floorboard.

"It's enough to boil your crabs, isn't it?"

"I don't think he knows. He couldn't just go along with it like that. And to think I left her a tip every time I went in there."

"How much?"

"Usually a quarter."

113

I wondered how many of those quarters had ended up at the Westside Liquor. "Well, to hell with the whole bunch of 'em," I said.

"I just don't think he knows."

"Don't be surprised at what people can do."

* * * * *

Ed and I kept to ourselves where we worked out in the young walnut orchard. In the evening when we came in, we would see the forklift driver loading the eighteen-wheelers with full bins of prunes. He was a high-school math teacher on summer vacation, and he came to work at ten every day. He wore red T-shirts and a white hard hat. Woody didn't wear a hard hat when he sat in the little scale house, but if he went out into the loading area he put one on. This was the first farm or ranch job I had ever had where anyone wore a hard hat, but that was more of Laketree's doing, like the accident prevention signs and the anti-depredation permits.

One day Ed and I ended up eating lunch at headquarters instead of out in the orchard because we had come in for a coil of hose. We sat at the picnic table in the shade of the syca-more trees and listened to Woody, Pat the mechanic, and the math teacher talk about queers.

The teacher was about forty and had a deep voice. He said that whenever he went into a bar where he thought there might be queers, he carried a twelve-inch crescent wrench in his pocket.

Woody added his two bits' worth. "Queers can be some of the best fighters you'll see."

"That's why I carry a wrench."

"I was in a bar once, and the guy next to me called one of 'em a queer to his face. So the queer said, 'There's two things I like to do. Suck dicks and fight.' And he beat the shit out of him."

The math teacher looked straight at Woody and nodded. "That's a favorite saying among queers."

"Maybe it is. I haven't been around 'em that much."

Ed had been quiet all this time, sullen-like, and now he blurted out. "Then why do you act like you know so much about 'em?"

Woody was calm as he gave Ed a frown. "I just know what I've seen. And I was in the Navy." He lit a cigarette and snapped his Zippo shut.

Ed's eyes got small, and he looked like a dog that was afraid of getting hit, but I could tell he took it as an offense that someone married to Claudette could talk like that. As for me, I didn't think there was very much that would have surprised me about that guy.

* * * * *

Ed stayed in a sulk for the rest of that day, and when I dropped by to pick him up the next morning, he said he didn't feel good enough to make it through a whole day. So I went to work without him. That evening I drove past the café, and I saw him sitting at the counter as if he lived there. I thought he might be getting ready to quit his job, but the next morning when I swung by his house he was ready.

Neither of us said anything as we left town on the two-lane highway. After a few minutes I saw a vehicle gaining on us. When I looked in the rear-view again, I saw that it was Benny's tan Ford pickup. Then it passed us, and I saw Woody on the passenger's side and Benny, in his khakis and jungle hat and dark glasses, behind the wheel. They both waved, and I thought they were an unlikely pair.

The pickup moved back into our lane as it left us behind. I glanced at Ed and asked, "What do you know about Claudette these days?"

He took on what I thought was a superior air. "I've got better things to do. We're gonna go to Sac this weekend. In Chet's Cad. We can meet girls there that don't have anything tyin' 'em down."

"Sometimes you wonder why women take up with the men they do."

Ed turned his head to look at me. "What do you mean?"

"Throwin' herself away on someone like him."

"Oh, yeah. If my sister went out with one of them, I'd make my parents kick her out of the house."

"No. I meant her husband."

"Oh, him."

"Guys like him, they don't appreciate a woman."

Ed had his lower lip stuck out. "It might do him some good if someone wised him up."

So that was where he was, I thought. He was feeding on it. He was worked up at the thought of Claudette doing it with a Mexican, and he couldn't admit that someone like Woody might look the other way. Ed was stuck on her, but he would like to see her get in trouble for what he thought she had done.

"I don't know," I said. "I'd rather not have anything to do with any of 'em." Of course I knew it was an easy thing for me to say at that point.

"Me neither. That's why I'm goin' to Sac."

* * * * *

We hadn't been pulling hoses for an hour that morning when Ed said he was going to take the pickup back to the yard.

"What for?" I asked.

"I've got to take a crap pretty bad."

I just about lost my patience. He was the only guy I knew who didn't carry paper with him. There were plenty of places along the edges of the orchards where a person would be out of the way, and every ranch pickup had at least one shovel in the back. I think he used the excuse sometimes just to get out of work.

"I hope you're not gone very long," I said. Once we had a two-man routine for pulling out the sprinkler hoses, it was a pain in the ass for one guy to have to do both parts.

"Just go there and back," he said.

I worked about an hour by myself until Ed showed up again. He parked the grey pickup at the end of the orchard and came walking my way. As soon as he got close, I could tell he was fuming. When I asked him what was eating on him, he said, "I can't believe how stubborn that guy is."

117

"Which guy?"

"Woody."

"What about?"

"He says his wife wouldn't do a thing like that."

"Oh, so you told him."

"And on top of that, he said Benny wouldn't be any kind of a friend if he did that."

"Well, I think Woody's a first-class sleaze."

"Do you think he'll tell Benny what I said?"

From the question, I thought Ed might be afraid of Benny. I shook my head. "I don't think so."

"But if they're friends?"

"Oh, don't count on it," I said. "I think our pal Woody's playing both ends against the middle, or something like that."

We went back to work, each of us on his own two rows, pulling hoses and setting sprinklers according to the pattern. About twenty minutes later, I happened to look in back of me and saw Benny's Ford pickup creeping along the edge of the orchard where Ed had parked the old grey Chevy. It was about nine-thirty in the morning, and the day was starting to warm up. I was surprised to see Benny's vehicle because he didn't have much call to come out to this part of the ranch. Besides, prune harvest was in full swing, and he should have been with the shaking crew out on the east side, with firm, fresh prunes rattling off his hard hat.

But there it was, the tan Ford with the aluminum camper shell on back. It went past the row I was working on, turned into the orchard, and headed in our direction. I paused with the sprinkler hose in my hands. I was impressed with how quiet the large area was and how all I could hear was the soft thump of the pickup as it rolled along on the uneven ground. The interior of the cab was in shadow, but I could make out the jungle helmet and a pair of dark glasses. The pickup turned almost sideways and came to a stop.

A thin, dark object poked out the window on the driver's side, and I heard a *blap*. Ed let out a yelp, and I saw him grab the upper part of his left arm. The *blap* sounded again, and everything that was ever laughable about Ed disappeared when a red spot flashed on his cheek and he went down like a sack of potatoes.

I dropped the black rubber hose and ducked behind a tree, but the trunk was only a couple of inches thick, and I knew I didn't have any real cover. I heard a *whiff* in the air near my head, followed by the *blap*, and I knew someone was shooting a .22 at me.

The pickup moved forward and was coming my way on the left, so I broke into a run to the right. I cut a diagonal through the orchard, then turned to my left and cut back the other way toward the old grey pickup. I heard the *whiff* and *blap* behind me one more time. As I got to the Chevy pickup, I looked back and saw Benny's Ford turning across one row and headed back my way.

I was heaving big breaths. I yanked open the door of the Chevy and jumped in, but the key was gone from the ignition.

I jumped out and ran around to the other side. Peeking across the back of the cab, I saw the tan Ford lumbering toward me. I reached into the bed of the Chevy, grabbed a field hoe, and took off again on a run. I headed for an overgrown

119

area, a kind of jungle of oak trees, grape vines, and elderberry bushes that grew along a bank of the old river bottom.

The grey pickup sat about fifty yards away, and beyond it, the tan Ford was crawling my way. I heard a noise now, a thumping noise and then a snap. The Ford stopped, and the thumping died. The door opened, and the jungle helmet caught the sunlight as the driver got out of the cab and bent down to look underneath the pickup.

I realized the Ford had come down the lane where I had been setting out sprinklers, and it must have caught one sprinkler or a pair and snapped the hose from the valve on the pipeline. I had seen one of the high-school kids wrap a hose around the blades of his mower, and I imagined something like that had happened with the drive line of the pickup. That would have caused the thumping sound.

The man in the helmet was on all fours now, with his back to me. I thought this was the time to make my move.

I came out of the jungle area crouching, and I kept the grey pickup between me and the other vehicle as I ran to the front fender of the Chevy. When I peeked up, I saw that the man was still on all fours, pulling on a length of black hose.

I got my hoe into position as I ran up behind him. I thought, no son of a bitch was going to make a loser out of me. I came to a stop as the man was pushing up on all fours, and I gave a swing with all my might.

The head of the hoe came down on the back edge of the helmet, flipping it aside and knocking the fellow off balance. Then he came up and turned, and I saw his face. It was paler than I expected, because it was the face of Woody Hudspeth.

I drew back to swing again, and he charged me. He drove his left shoulder into my chest and knocked me down, then grabbed me by the shirt and punched me solid on the left side of my head. He stood over me, took hold of my shirt with both hands, picked me up, and slammed me to the ground. My head scraped the dirt and made my hat fall away, so he got an easy grab on my hair and punched me another time.

As I hit the ground again, I thought, *I've got to get away from this.* I rolled over onto all fours, and he kicked me where my chest meets my ribs. I grabbed the hoe handle, and he reached over me to try to take hold of it. I slammed my elbow back into his chin, then pulled on the hoe handle and drove the tip of it into the pit of his stomach. That relaxed his hold on me, so I crawled forward, dragging the hoe.

I rose to my feet and turned in a half-circle, swinging the hoe. It glanced off his shoulder. As I stepped back I re-grouped, and this time I fetched him a wallop behind his left ear, and he went down. That was when I lost control. I hit him again and again and again, bringing the heavy steel shank of the hoe head down onto the base of his skull. Everything else in the world went away, and I was by myself in a distant walnut orchard clobbering a man who had tried to kill me.

* * * * *

I was in jail for two months. It took that long for the cops and the D.A. to decide that Woody had a motive, twisted though it was, for framing Benny, and that I didn't have a motive beyond looking out for myself, even though I took it way farther

121

John D. Nesbitt

than I had to. If I had anything to be glad about, it was being able to say, in all truth, that I hadn't had anything to do with Claudette. And I got grilled about it more than once.

When I got out, the days were shorter and the first rains of October had come. A lot of the field work was done, and I was flat broke. Thanks to the cops, my car had been towed and impounded, and the storage fee alone was more than the car was worth. My room at the Travelers Court had long been cleaned out, and nobody could tell me where my stuff was. So I had a rough go of it for a few days. I got a job stripping shingles off a barn, and then I found work raking walnuts ahead of a pick-up machine,

I bumped into Claudette, of all places, in the second-hand store. I was buying an old corduroy coat, and she was looking at women's clothes.

"So you're still around," she said.

"I just got out." I could tell she didn't want to talk to me, but I thought I had a right to say something. "It was a lot of trouble," I said.

"Yeah,"

"I guess it was too bad about Woody—I mean, what happened to him. But he didn't have any call to do what he did."

"And all for no reason," she said. She must have sensed a need to try to convince me, because she went on to say, "I never did anything with Benny. I never would have."

I didn't have an answer for that. I said, "Well, it's too bad about Ed. He didn't ever do any harm to anyone." I imagined

122

him in Chet's Cad, the two of them speeding down the free-way to Sacramento, toward girls I couldn't quite picture. As a kind of afterthought I said, "He was all right."

"Uh-huh."

I thought she was going to say something else, and when she didn't, I said, "Do you still work at the Wagon Wheel?"

"Nah. I had to leave there."

I nodded. "Well, I guess I'll see you around."

"Sure."

I paid for my coat, walked outside, and put it on. I had three dollars and a little bit of change, but I figured the least I could do was go have a cup of coffee and put a quarter in the jukebox.

Boom-Boom

When I sort back through it all, I think of the Kilmer place where it began. The bare ground was rolled flat, and the trees were dry as well, with the hulls on the almonds splitting open and turning grey, ready to fall. When we would get there in the morning, the air was still and cool. Then the hustle began as the two crews got started. Each crew had a tractor to pull the two sleds, plus a second tractor that had the shaker boom mounted on it. Every time we knocked two trees and rolled up the canvas sheets, the driver gunned the engine and pulled forward to the next two trees. While he went back for the shaker, the other kid and I pulled out the sheets again. Then came the shaking, which up close sounded like a giant jack-hammer but from across the orchard sounded like a machine gun.

All day long there was noise from the equipment, plus voices from the workers. Dust came up from the ground and down from the trees, and the temperature went over a hundred every day. We had plenty to do just to manage the sheets and the fallen almonds, hit a few licks with a mallet or pole, then shovel the load into burlap sacks when the sled got full. I didn't pay any attention to the other crew or to the two swamp-ers, who showed up on the third day.

We had been leaving sacks standing in groups of six or seven, until Kilmer got started with the swampers. He drove his dark blue Ford pickup and pulled a low trailer while the two husky guys, probably in their mid-twenties, loaded the sacks. Back at the huller they dumped the sacks, then came back for more.

We finished the first variety late that afternoon, and we sat in the shade of a big walnut tree in the boss's yard while he went inside and figured our pay. When he came out with the checks, he told the other kid and me that we could ride back to town with the two guys who had come that day. The boss had been picking us up in the morning and taking us back in the evening, and he said he would come for us again in a couple of days when the next variety was ready. We had already seen the green hulls starting to split and turn yellow, so I knew what he meant.

I knew what it meant for me, too. This kid Dennis was still living with his parents, so he could sit in front of the cooler and watch t.v. for a couple of days. I was out knocking around on my own, though, and two days off meant two days without wages. It wasn't enough time to go find another job until Kilmer started up again, so I either sat it out or found another job, period.

The swampers had a 1955 faded red-and-white Pontiac, and on the way into town they struck up a conversation. The one driving, who was red-haired, looked in the mirror and asked our names. Dennis gave his name, and I told him mine. Then the guy riding shotgun, who had dark hair, turned around and asked us if we wanted to drink some beer.

We both said sure.

"Let's do it this way," he said. "We each put in a dollar, and we'll have enough for two six-packs. That's enough for three each."

Dennis said that was fine, and I said it was all right with me.

The guy in the dark hair bought two six-packs of Schlitz in the can. I hadn't drunk it before, but when you're under age you drink what you get, so I took my can and pulled off the ring and tab.

"Don't lift it up till we're out of town," said the red-haired guy. He drove out on the old highway until we came to a wide spot where there were some oak trees, and he pulled over.

The beer tasted good—kind of watery and tinny, but it had a cold bite to it. The two guys in front lit up cigarettes, and Dennis bummed one. Then he asked them their names.

"Floyd," said the red-head.

"Mine's Benson," said his pal.

"Are those your first names?" Dennis asked.

"Last names." Benson blew smoke out through his nose. "We were in the Army, and you get used to goin' by your last name. You boys been called up yet?"

"Not yet," said Dennis. "I just graduated."

"Me neither," I said.

"Maybe you'll get lucky and not have to go." Benson took a swallow of beer. "What are you two goin' to do for the next while? Gonna wait for this farmer to come around when he gets ready?"

Dennis huffed on his cigarette. "I guess. How about you guys?"

Benson did a move where he turned down his mouth and shook his head. "We don't do this kind of work," he said. "But we needed gas money."

"What kind of work do you do?" I asked.

"Construction. Why, hell, even kids like you can make two, maybe three times what you make workin' in the dirt."

I was getting interested. "Where do you find work like that?"

Benson gave a wag of the head. "You've got to go where they're building. Right now, there's a boom in Redding."

"That's not so far," said Dennis. "What are they building?"

"Houses, apartments."

"And you guys find work, just like that?"

Benson nodded toward his pal. "He's a framer, and I'm an electrician. We can work in one trade or the other. I follow him, or he follows me. Unless we find work in both. Are you two ready?" He held up an unopened can.

We finished off our beers, and Benson handed us each a new one. Dennis smoked another cigarette and asked more questions. Benson said he was from Pittsburgh, and Floyd said he was from Oklahoma and might be related to Pretty Boy Floyd the outlaw. Dennis got their first names out of them, too. Benson was Bill, and Floyd was Larry. I was sitting on the passenger's side, kind of out of the way, and I didn't have the habit of asking questions, so I just drank my beer.

Benson turned to me and said, "You don't talk much. What did you say your name was?"

"Stan."

"Stan what?"

"Campbell."

"Like soup."

"I guess."

Benson had a heavy face and small eyes, but he opened up when he smiled. "You kids look like you know how to work."

Dennis was taking a drink, so I answered. "I'd say I do."

"Well, shit," said Benson. "Redding's not that far. If you kids want to ride up there with us, we can split the gas, get a room for all four, and see what's goin' on." He looked at his partner, who nodded.

"Might as well," said Dennis. He looked at me. "How about you?"

I shrugged. "I'm not doin' anything else. My room rent comes up tomorrow."

"What kind of room is it?" asked Benson.

"Just a regular room in an old travel court."

"Huh. Why don't you let us stay there tonight, and we can all leave in the morning? Get there during the day and look around." He held up two more cans of Schlitz.

"I guess so." I took a beer.

"Let you kids learn how to make some money. And don't worry. We'll get some more beer, too."

* * * * *

I had a headache in the morning, and these other two guys

weren't moving very fast, so the car was hot inside and stale-smelling when we got ready to go. Floyd was driving again, and I gave him directions on how to get to Dennis's house.

Dennis came out looking uncomfortable. He stood at the passenger's side, squinting in the sun, and said, "I've decided not to go."

Benson flicked his ashes out the window. "That's okay," he said. "We'll send you a postcard, and pictures of all the girls."

In a few more minutes, we were on the freeway headed north to Redding. We were whipping along at seventy in their old Pontiac with the windows down and the radio turned up. The two guys in front hollered back and forth when they had something to say, and they pretty much left me alone. I had the back seat to myself and my canvas bag, and I watched the dry countryside go by. It seemed like nothing but star thistles and sour dock, both dry at that time of year. At about noontime I began to see trees, tall and broad-leafed, and then we took an off-ramp into Redding.

I was getting hungry, and I imagined the other guys were too, since we hadn't had any breakfast. I wondered if they were going to pull into a hamburger joint until Benson said, "This looks like a good place," and Floyd brought the Pontiac to a stop in front of a bar.

Benson spoke to me over his shoulder. "We're goin' to go in here for a minute and see what's the haps about work around this place."

"I'm startin' to get hungry," I said.

John D. Nesbitt

"That's all right. We won't be long. You keep an eye on the car, and we'll get something to eat in a little while."

I sat in that car sweating as I waited from one minute to the next. At least a dozen times I thought about getting out and leaving, but I couldn't quite get up the nerve. I figured that if I went in and told Floyd and Benson I was taking off, they'd tell me to go back to the car and wait. If I left without saying anything, they'd be good and pissed that I didn't keep an eye on the car, and they might even come looking for me. So I sat there for about two hours until they came out of the bar.

"What did you find out?" I asked.

Floyd slid in behind the wheel. "Not worth a shit."

Benson didn't say anything.

"Are we going to get something to eat?" I asked.

"Sure," said Benson. "We'll eat."

Floyd pulled out onto the road and headed towards the main part of town. About a half-mile later, I saw a place on the right called Winkler's Patio. It was painted pale yellow and had white lattice-work along a roofed outdoor sitting area.

"There's a place," I said.

I thought we were going to go past it, but Floyd cut the wheel and hung a right into the front lot, where the car came to a stop.

When the two guys in front just sat there, I said, "I don't think they've got any car hops."

"No, of course they don't have any car hops," said Benson. "Not in this shit-knockin' place." He spit out the window. "I don't care if we eat or not."

130

"Well, I'm hungry," I said.

Floyd opened his door. "Let's eat."

I guessed they had some kind of a disagreement back in the bar, but I didn't want that to keep me from getting lunch, so I opened my door.

"You two go ahead," said Benson, still in a grumble. "Don't take all day."

We ordered our food at the window inside the shaded area and sat down at a heavy steel picnic table. As we waited for the order, I asked Floyd if they had found out where the work was.

He had just lit a cigarette, and as he blew the smoke away he said, "There's no work here."

"None?"

"Not in this town. At least, there's no housing tracts being put in or apartment complexes goin' up." His face was relaxed, and his eyes looked dull. "There's damn sure not any boom goin' on."

When we got back to the car, Benson said, "Piss on this cow-town. Whoever said there was work here had his head up his ass."

Floyd made a big smile with his mouth closed. "You're the one said there was a boom here."

"I mean whoever said it to me. If I woulda known what a podunk town it is, I'd've laughed in his face."

"What do we do, then?" I asked.

Floyd had cranked up the car and was pulling out onto the road. As he looked over his left shoulder for traffic he said,

"We're gonna have to go somewhere else. I guess we can try what those guys in the bar said."

"What's that?"

"Portland. Even if these yokels don't know their ass from Shinola, there's bound to be work there."

"Sure there is," said Benson. He flicked his cigarette butt out the window. "Waste our time in this two-bit town, any-way."

* * * * *

The air coming in the windows was hot and dry, and after one big grasshopper smashed against my fingers, I kept my hand inside. Bumblebees and cicadas and butterflies and all kinds of bugs had splattered on the windshield. The radio was turned off, and the two guys in front weren't talking much. They had a six-pack on the seat between them, and I had said I didn't care for any yet, so they were drinking the beer and smoking cigarettes as we rocketed north towards Oregon.

I could tell Floyd was letting things eat on him when he said, "Some boom."

"Aw, hell with it," said his pal.

"We come all this way because there's supposed to be a boom, and there's not shit."

"Piss on 'em, I say. We just keep goin'."

"To the next boom?"

Benson sniffed. "It was your idea just as much as mine to go to Portland."

"What are we supposed to do, go back?"

"You could."

"On what? We've got barely enough to get to Portland." Floyd looked at me in the mirror. "You've got something for gas, haven't you?"

I was wishing I had gotten out in Redding, but I said, "Yeah."

He looked as if he settled down a little, but he didn't let it go. Without even glancing at Benson he said, "We come six hundred miles because you believed there was a boom."

"You believed it, too."

"I took your word for it. Boom-boom."

"So there's not any work in that chickenshit town. We'll go where there is."

"To a boom in Portland."

"It's a hell of a lot closer than where we came from."

We stopped in a town called Dunsmuir, where I gave them ten dollars and they filled the tank. Then they got another six-pack, and we were out rolling along at seventy again. We were in the mountains by now, but the freeway was a good, broad highway, and Floyd kept his foot on the gas. As he took a drink from his new beer, he started in on Benson again.

"Boom-boom."

"Yeah, yeah, give me shit."

"Boom-Boom Benson. Knows where the work is. Ten dollars an hour."

"When we find work, you'll see."

"Just follow Boom-Boom Benson."

"Well, fuck it, then. Just go back."

"What do you mean, go back? The farther we go, the farther away we get."

"If you don't like it, go back."

"How in the hell do we go back?"

"Easy. Just do it." Without another word, Benson reached over to the gearshift on the steering column and pulled it down.

A sickening, grinding sound ran from the front floorboard all the way through the underside of the car and then changed to a clattering whir. The Pontiac started losing speed, and Floyd was pulling up on the gearshift, trying to yank it back into a forward gear. He pulled over to the side of the road and stopped, then jammed the gearshift into drive and gave the car some gas. It lurched forward, but no matter how much Floyd stepped on it, he couldn't get above fifteen miles an hour.

His eyes were wide open, and his face was red. "Look what you did to my car! What a fuckhead thing to do."

"Piss on it," said Benson. "You wanna go back, go back."

"I never said I wanted to."

"You give me shit about everything."

"I'll give you shit about this. You fucked up my car."

Benson scowled and said, "I can fuck up more than that."

Floyd gave him a funny look and didn't answer.

We were crawling along the shoulder at ten to fifteen miles an hour, and I was wondering what we were going to do next. The sensible thing would have been for me to get out, carry my bag across the highway, and hitch-hike back to the valley. But I had a sick feeling in my guts, and I felt as if I couldn't make myself move. Along with that, I had the idea that my ten dollars were in the gas tank. That was a wrong idea, because the ten dollars weren't mine anymore, but I didn't think in those terms. So I stayed where I was in the back seat and said, "Hell with it, I'll have a beer, too."

Benson didn't seem to care for that, but he gave me one anyway.

We threw out the empties as we went along, and the beer was all gone by the time we limped into a town called Weed. It was early evening. The mosquitoes were out, and the only service station in town was closed. We pulled in back of it and sat in the car and slapped mosquitoes. The sun went down, and I drifted in and out of sleep. The other two guys shifted in their seats and slept, too. And still it did not occur to me that I could have just up and left. I felt that I was tied to these two guys.

* * * * *

Just before daylight a cop rapped on the window, and Floyd rolled it down. He told the cop we had had car trouble and were waiting for the Enco station to open. The cop said we had to move, and he told Floyd there was a café open across the street from the station and we should go there.

I ordered a stack of hotcakes, and so did Floyd. Benson had a short stack. We drank coffee for about an hour and a half, and when the service station had been open a while, we got in the car and drove back across the street. Floyd went in and talked to the owner, and after a while he came out and gave us the news.

"This guy says it's goin' to be about three hundred dollars."

"Hell, we don't have that," said Benson.

"That's what I told him. I asked him if he could patch it up. He said he won't do anything half-assed. He either redoes the transmission, or he doesn't touch it."

Benson rapped a cigarette against his lighter and then lit it. "Well, I guess we don't have much choice."

We got back out on the highway and crawled along at that slow pace for what seemed like an eternity. Floyd had gotten a road map, so Benson studied it. We were still in the mountains until we got into Oregon, and then we dropped down into a valley. We were in farming country again, and I didn't feel so lost. Where there were crops, there was work.

We stopped in Ashland, where a man in all khakis let us put water in the radiator. He said the place to go was Medford, just up the road a ways. We could find work there, picking pears.

We crept into Medford before the labor office closed, and we got a referral to a place out east of town where we could stay in the bunkhouse and ride with the crew. Benson didn't like it much, but it sounded good to me. Everything was right there—food, a place to stay, transportation. Floyd could see the benefit of it, too. He said he was willing to give it a try.

* * * * *

The weather felt chilly the first morning, and the hard green pears were cold to the touch. The three of us were picking into one bin, using twelve-foot ladders and canvas picking bags, the kind that unhooked at the bottom and dropped open. I was back in my own world now, and I was glad to show these guys how to go about ringing the pears for size, pushing up on the stem, hoisting the bag, setting the ladder, and on and on. Floyd got the hang of it pretty well, but Benson hated it.

"This is shit for work," he said. He was sitting on the third rung of his ladder, resting his forearms on the leather ridge that ran around the top of the picking bag. He had lit a cigarette, so his partner stopped to join him. I paused for a minute, too.

"It's what we're stuck with until we've got money to leave on," said Floyd. "The more of these tubs we fill, the more we make."

"Tubs, my ass."

"That's what the row boss calls 'em. I don't give a damn myself. Five bucks is five bucks. Watch how this kid does it."

"Looks like he was born to it. Is that right, Slats?"

"Not quite," I said. He had taken to calling me Slats, I think because I had thin arms and hadn't gotten my muscle yet.

"Well, I wasn't," said Benson. He flicked his ashes to one side, sniffed, and spit.

I went back to my tree and started picking bottoms. I wasn't going to leave all the easy picking for Benson, even if he got off his ass. Floyd went back to working on his own tree, and when I went to empty into the bin, he did, too.

Benson was still sitting on the rung of his ladder, smoking another Marlboro. He said, "Son of a bitch, Slats. You got twice as many in your bag as Floyd does. This is your kind of work, isn't it?"

I didn't stop to talk. I was snapping the bottom of my bag into place as I walked past him. I think I had my courage up because I was in my element and he wasn't. "I don't like to be called Slats," I said.

The whole deal with fruit picking, or any kind of piece work, is to get as much done as you can in the cool part of the day. None of it is fun, but the time goes by a hell of a lot better if you buckle down and work, not stand around and lolly-gag. When I came up with my next bag, Floyd had about two-thirds of a bag to dump alongside me. Benson was still smoking his cigarette.

"Come on," said Floyd. "We can't let this kid pick more than the two of us together."

"Maybe that's his talent. What do you think, kid?"

"I don't know anything about talent. You just do it."

Benson dropped the stub of his cigarette and stepped on it as he stood up. "I guess so," he said.

As he went to picking his tree, I thought, if we were some- where else, he'd want to hit me.

* * * * *

After a couple of days of picking pears, we got a draw for twenty dollars each, which was just about all we had coming when you figured room and board. We got into the old red-orange Pontiac and started for town. We didn't have anything in particular to do, like laundry, but these other two guys got antsy sitting around the labor camp. We poked along at fifteen miles an hour, and when we got into town we went to a liquor store.

Benson came out with a fifth of rum and two quarts of Coke. He got in, and Floyd started to drive out to the country where we could drink in the car. We went past a car lot, and there in the second row was a nice, clean '56 Chevy, aqua blue and white.

"That's what we need," said Benson.

Floyd answered, "No shit."

Out past the edge of town, we drank about a third of each of the Coke bottles and then poured in the rum. Then we drank the rum and Coke, and the whole mess was gone by the time the sun was going down.

"We ought to get some more cigarettes," said Benson.

Floyd started the car, and we puttered back to town.

As we went past the car lot, Benson said, "Why don't you loan me that ignition key?"

"What for?"

"A lot of these GM keys will open the doors of other cars."

With those GM cars of the 1950's you could also take the key out of the ignition while the engine was running, so Floyd gave his pal the key and pulled over.

"Just drive around back," said Benson.

We did that, and a couple of minutes later the clean '56 Chevy came rolling up next to us.

139

"Son of a bitch," said Floyd. "He hot-wired it."

Benson leaned over and cranked down the window. "Follow me out to where we were," he said.

He took off, and when we got to the place where we had drunk the rum and Coke, he was waiting for us. In a few minutes he and Floyd put the California plates on the blue-and-white Chevy and the Oregon plates on the Pontiac we had been traveling in.

"We didn't get the cigarettes," said Benson.

He drove the Chevy, and Floyd went with him. I waited in the front seat of the old crippled Pontiac, wondering what the hell I would tell a cop if one came along.

It wasn't but a couple of miles into town, but those two guys took almost an hour. As I sat there, I tried to imagine how I could get away from them. I sure couldn't drive away in their car, and if I got out and walked back to the labor camp, they would catch up with me either on the road or at the bunk-house. So I sat there on the passenger side of the car with the stolen plates on it.

When the guys came back, they had two girls with them, all four in the front seat.

Floyd got out, and Benson drove off with the two girls.

"What's going on?" I asked as Floyd scooted in behind the wheel.

He started the car and put it in gear. "We picked up these two girls. They wanted us to buy booze for 'em, and we said we would if they'd drink with us. So they got a pint of sloe gin, and we got two six-packs. They know of a place to park."

"What kind of girls are they?"

He looked over at me. "I think they're all right. The one sittin' next to Benson has a boyfriend overseas, so I think she's itchy. Her girlfriend's along for the ride, but she might be okay, too."

We drove a couple of miles until the road crossed a creek, and on the other side, down on the right, we could see parking lights. Floyd pulled down into the spot, where the ground was bumpy and gravelly with weeds growing up in some places and smashed down where cars had turned around. Benson was sitting in the front seat of the Chevy with the two girls. They were all smoking cigarettes.

Everyone got out and stood around. The girls had already started on their sloe gin, and Benson was drinking a bottle of Olympia. Floyd got one for himself and one for me.

Those girls were eighteen at the most, and the liquor went to their heads pretty quick. The one with the boyfriend over-seas was named Bev, and her favorite expression was "Whoop-dee-shit." Her girlfriend's name was Carol. She didn't talk as much. Benson was putting his arm around Bev, and Floyd was making the same kind of move on Carol.

Benson started spinning a story about how he and Floyd were from Coos Bay, which I guess he got off the map. He said they'd been down in California and made a bunch of money in the oilfields, and that's how they got the nice car. They were going to sell the other one to me, and then they were going on to Alaska to work on the pipeline.

"Well, whoop-dee-shit," said Bev. "I'll go with you."

"Why not?" said Benson. "The both of ya can go." He flicked away a live cigarette butt, and it landed in the gravel.

"How about it?" asked Floyd. He gave Carol's shoulder a squeeze.

"I don't know. I have to pee."

"Do you need some help?"

"Not from you. Bev, come with me."

"You don't need me."

"Come with me."

"Oh, okay." Bev dropped her cigarette and took a couple of stabs at it with her sandal until she snuffed it. Then she went with her girlfriend into the willows.

It was not a very bright night, but I could see them walking away, unsteady-like, in their shorts and sleeveless blouses. They were both blondes, and Bev wore her hair poofed up on top more than Carol did. She also had more of a figure, with boobs that pooked out. When the girls came back, I could tell them apart easy enough, and when they got into the same arrangement with the two guys, I could tell no one was going to pay attention to me.

Not only was I the odd man out, but my nerves were eating on me about the whole thing. Here we were with a stolen car and two girls that might be under eighteen, and we had to go to work in the morning. Naturally, no one had said anything about picking pears, and I think the other two guys had had enough to drink that it took the edge off of any sense of responsibility. Maybe if I had drunk more and was going after one of the girls I might have been the same. I don't know. As it was, I just stood around and fidgeted.

The four of them chattered on, with Benson and Floyd making plenty of suggestive remarks, and finally they got the two girls separated. Carol was blubbering by now, and Floyd got her into the front seat of the Chevy, while Benson got the other girl around to the back door of the Pontiac.

"Whoop-dee-shit," she said just before she got in. "I can do what I want. I know he's over there screwin' gooks."

I wandered off to the edge of the parking area, wondering if there was any way I could get back to the labor camp by myself, when in the hell these other guys were going to get around to it, and what they were going to do with the '56 Chevy.

A car door opened, and I heard Floyd call my name. The interior light had not come on, but I could see him standing by the driver's door of the clean-looking Chevy. I walked to the front of the car, and he came as far as the fender. His voice was low and clear in the darkness.

"She says she'll do it with me, but she doesn't want to do it with everyone else around, so I'm going to take her down the road, and then we'll come back."

I shrugged. By now I was pissed at all the delay, as well as on edge about when a cop was going to show up, but I knew how much my opinion counted. So I said, "I guess I'll just wait, then. It's what I'm doing anyway."

"Okay," he said, still in a low voice. "If the others ask anything, tell 'em I'll be right back."

He got into the car, closed the door with a muffled click, and got the engine going. It had a quiet purr. He turned the car around and eased out of there, and the headlights didn't come on until he was up on the main road.

I heard some commotion from the back seat of the other car. Bev was saying, "Don't, don't, not now," and then her voice got louder as she called out Carol's name.

Benson's voice came out rough as he said, "Calm down, damn it. Just do this."

"I don't want to."

"You said you did."

"Carol!"

"Don't worry about her. She's got her hands full. Just lay back and enjoy it."

"Umph! No!"

I heard a wrestling sound, of bodies rubbing the upholstery and making the seat springs crumple.

Benson's voice was sharp now as he said, "Settle down!"

The girl said, "I want out."

Then there was more thrashing, and it sounded like two people hitting each other.

Bev's voice sounded like she was struggling. "Uh! Ahh!"

"Knock it off!" said Benson.

There was a short lull, and she said, "You're a fuck-nut." Then there was grunting and groaning, and I could tell she was trying to get out of the car.

I heard him give her three or four whacks, and there was more bumping around. Then it sounded like he hit her pretty solid, and everything went quiet. I had a sick feeling in my stomach, but I couldn't help watching to see what was going to happen. In the faint moonlight I saw Benson back his way out of the car, pull up his pants, and stand up straight.

I listened for the sound of the girl crying, but I didn't hear a thing. Now I was scared deep. My head was buzzing, and a strange, hollow feeling went all the way to my feet.

Benson leaned into the back seat for almost a minute and then came out and took a deep breath. "Stupid bitch," he said.

I stood in the dark about fifteen feet away and waited for him to say something else. When he didn't, I fought the dryness in my mouth and said, "What happened?"

His voice had a quaver in it, and I could tell he was trying to make light of things. "Oh, she got all shook up about her friend leaving, and I tried to get her to settle down."

After another silence I said, "It didn't sound good."

He cleared his throat. "It wasn't. Or it isn't. Where in the hell's Larry, anyway?"

"He went off with the other girl. He said he'd be back."

"That's a hell of a mess. Did he think he was goin' to get somethin'?"

"I guess so."

"Dumb shit. And we're stuck here with this on our hands."

I didn't know what time it was, but I figured it was close to ten. Floyd hadn't been gone that long, and I wondered what we were going to do when he came back with the drunk girl. I was fearing the worst about the girl in the back seat of the Pontiac, and besides that, I was worried about the stolen car. Underneath that huge, dark sky, it seemed as if everything, the whole world, had gone way out of whack, yet I still had it in mind that we had to pick pears in the morning.

Benson lit a cigarette. "Shit," he said. "He's got all the beer with him, too. I could use one about now."

We stood in the gravel as he smoked his cigarette. No sound came from the old Pontiac. The back door was open just as he had left it, but he didn't go near it. He took a long drag on the cigarette, and it glowed in the dark. "Why don't you go close that door," he said.

I would have given anything to be able to say no, but I went and pushed the door shut.

After what seemed like an hour but was probably less, I saw headlights coming down the road. Brake lights went on as the car crossed the bridge, and then the front beams swung down to where we were. I told myself that if it wasn't Floyd, I was going to have to decide pretty quick what I was going to say.

It was Floyd, though, and he didn't have anyone in the front seat with him. When he stopped, I went to the driver's window and looked in to see if the girl was passed out in the back seat, but she wasn't.

"Where's the girl?" I asked.

Floyd shut off the lights and killed the engine. "I had to take her to town. She was sloppy drunk and wouldn't do anything. Did Bill get any?"

"You'll have to ask him."

Casual-like, Floyd opened the door and got out. I followed him around to the other side of the Pontiac, where Benson stood with his back to the car.

"What took so long?" he asked.

146

"I had to take her to town. She was drunk off her ass. Where's the other one?"

"In there."

"Is she passed out?"

"No, I think it's worse. Pretty bad scene, actually."

Floyd's answer came quick. "What do you mean?"

"Well, um, things didn't go well." Benson took out a cigarette, rapped it on his lighter, and lit it. "I was startin' to get it on, and then you took off with the other girl, and this one got worked up. Didn't want to go any farther, even after she said she would. I told her to cool it, and she wouldn't, and I think I hit her too hard."

I could tell he was trying to make the fight itself seem like less than it was.

"Did you knock her out?" Floyd asked.

"Worse, I think."

Floyd seemed to get it then. He took a seething breath. "You stupid son of a bitch. How could you do that?"

"I didn't hit her that hard, or it didn't seem like it. But she was twistin' around, and all cramped in the back seat. I think she cricked her neck."

"You mean you did. You stupid fucker. How could you do something so god-damn stupid?"

Benson's voice came back pretty sharp. He was done making excuses. "Look. It just happened, that's what. I wasn't trying to hurt her. I just wanted to finish."

Things went silent for a moment until Floyd shook his head and said, "I'm goin' to get a beer."

"Get me one, too. Do you want one, kid?"

"Sure."

Floyd came back with three bottles of Oly with the caps all off. "This is so fucked-up I can't believe it," he said as he handed out the beers. "It doesn't make any sense at all. I mean, this is really—it's crazy. What in the hell are we gonna do?"

Benson took a long swallow. I could tell he had pulled himself together when he said, "It's a cinch we can't leave her here. This is the first place they'll come tomorrow morning."

Floyd stared at him. "You want to hide it, then."

"I sure as hell ain't gonna turn myself in and get thrown in the jug, not if there's a way out."

"What's that?"

"I'd say we get rid of it and the car at the same time."

"My car?"

"Yeah, this one that doesn't run worth a shit."

"Just leave it somewhere?"

"Not just anywhere. But it sure doesn't make sense to take it with us. And if we leave it in sight, with or without these Oregon plates, it's a matter of time till they run a serial number and connect a name with it. Even if the car doesn't have anything in it, they connect it with the missing girl."

"My name."

I could tell he resented it, but there was worry in his voice as well.

"That's if they find it," Benson said. "But if we put it where they can't find it, we can be long gone. We take the Oregon plates off and keep 'em, and later we put 'em back on the new car and leave it in the middle of a city."

"So where do we put the Pontiac?"

Benson took another drink. "There's lakes and reservoirs up the ass around here. I saw 'em on the map."

"Where's the map?"

"It's in the glove box."

"The dome light doesn't work in that Chevy."

"I know. We can read it with a match or a lighter. To begin with, we'll read it in this car." Benson pointed at the Pontiac.

"I don't want to sit in there when she's in the back seat."

"Jesus Christ," said Benson. "I'll put her in the trunk. That's where she's got to go anyway."

I went off by myself and turned my back. For the ump-teenth time I wished I could get the hell away from there, but I couldn't imagine how. I heard the trunk open, then close about a minute later. Next I heard a car door close and two others open. I looked and saw Floyd and Benson reading the map inside the old Pontiac.

After a little while, the car doors closed and Floyd called my name. He and Benson were standing between the two cars, and I walked up within speaking distance.

"Here's the deal," said Floyd. He pointed at the Chevy. "Bill's gonna drive this car to lead the way. I'll ride with him and read the map. You can drive the other car and follow. You don't have to see anything or know anything, just drive it until we get to where we want to get rid of it. Then you're in the clear. Even if we get stopped, none of this is yours. We'll keep you out of it."

I took a deep breath. Even though I thought he was talking to me like I was the biggest dummy in the world, it was one way to get out of this mess. I didn't want to drive a car with a dead body in the trunk, but at least I couldn't see it, and I sure didn't want to ride in the stolen car with Bill Benson and read the road map to him. Even if I had preferred that, I didn't feel like I had much choice.

"Okay," I said.

He handed me the key. For a second I wondered why he had taken it out of the ignition, but maybe he wanted to make a show of giving it to me. I didn't know. I got in, started the car, and waited. They got into the Chevy and led the way out of the make-out spot. A minute later I was topping out at fifteen miles an hour and clutching the wheel as I bent over it. I felt as if I'd been up all night, but I knew it wasn't that late yet.

I followed the blue-and-white Chevy for a long time until it pulled over. I stopped behind it. Benson got out, shielding his eyes from the headlights, and came back to my window.

"This is goin' too slow," he said. "We're gonna go see if we can find a rope or a tow chain," he said. "You just keep movin' along, and we'll catch up with you again."

I felt I was really stuck now. My fingerprints were all over this car, so even if I got out and left it on the side of the road, I was connected. And the dread in my guts told me I didn't want to cross these two guys at this point. At the same time, I knew they wanted to ditch the car, and I doubted they would just leave me wandering like a goose in the moonlight. They had their own asses to look out for. I told myself that if

I got stopped, I wasn't going to take the rap for them, but deeper down I knew that I would be taking some kind of a rap, regardless, if we got caught.

"Okay," I said. "I don't know where I am, though."

"Just stay on this road."

He got into the Chevy and took off, and I got going at a crawl again. Now the time seemed to really drag. I remember seeing an old black highway sign that read Upper Klamath Lake, but the reflectors had been pitted out, and I couldn't see how far it was.

A long time later, a car came up fast behind me and then slowed as it went around. It was the shiny '56 Chevy with the black-and-yellow California plates. It came to a stop up ahead, so I pulled in behind it.

Floyd got out of the passenger's side with a heap of grey rope in his hands. He walked through the headlights and came around to my side.

"We found a rope," he said.

I could imagine him prowling around in someone's barn-yard.

"We're goin' to tie onto you and see if we can't make better time. Pull up a little more. When we get goin', leave it in neutral."

He got us tied together with a double strand, and as the cars eased out onto the highway, the rope jerked and thumped. I made sure I was in neutral. Little by little we picked up speed, and pretty soon we were jamming along at sixty miles an hour. I had the steering wheel clamped in a death grip, and still the car pulled to one side or the other. I kept my right foot ready to stomp on the brake if I had to.

It was a nerve-wracking ride, and it didn't help me forget about the dead girl. I had the feeling that she was riding on my back as I careened along, drifting from side to side as the shiny stolen Chevy yanked me through the night.

We must have gone thirty or forty miles that way until the rope broke and I was left coasting. The blue-and-white car stayed well ahead, braking now and then, until I rolled to a stop. The other car backed up, and Floyd got out. He looked at the broken rope hanging from the back bumper of the Chevy, and he got on his hands and knees to look under the car I was driving. Then he got up and came around to my window.

"Well, that's the end of that," he said. "Just follow like before. We've got about another ten miles."

I crept along for another forty-five minutes and then followed them as they turned off the highway onto a dirt road at my left. There was a sign that said something like Thornton or Boynton Reservoir. I followed the other car into the dark night until we came to a high spot overlooking a body of water.

Floyd got out again and said, "I'll take it from here. Let's roll down all four windows, and we'll pick you up on our way out."

I was more than glad to stand by myself in the dark, with my back to the water. I heard the noise of the two cars, one louder than the other, and after a while I heard just the quieter one coming toward me.

I turned to face it, and when it pulled up, I opened the back door and got in. Once we were out on the highway, I let out a long breath. Even riding in a stolen car was a relief, compared to being dragged through the night, hunched over the steering wheel with my hands cramped, knowing every second of the way that the dead girl was in the trunk behind me. Now the calmness was unreal, and I couldn't be sure that the nightmare was over.

Floyd tried to tune in a radio station while Benson lead-footed it back towards Medford. Time seemed to speed up as the bushes and posts and dirt banks flowed by in the darkness.

When we were back into the orchard country, Benson pulled over and called a piss stop. He cut the lights down to parking, and we all stepped out into the night. The moon hadn't brightened things any more than before, and I had no idea of what time it was.

"Where are we?" I asked.

Benson answered. "The turn-off to the labor camp is about two miles ahead on the right."

Something in his voice made me wonder. "What's the plan?" I asked. "Why did we stop?"

Benson sounded impatient, and he talked down to me as always. "We stopped to take a piss. The plan is that we've got to get the hell out of here just as soon as we can get our stuff."

"Which way?"

"Depends."

"Depends on what?"

"On which way we turn."

153

It sounded like he didn't want to tell me any more than he had to. Maybe he thought I wouldn't want to go along and he'd deal with me when the time came. It gave me the feeling that I was one more thing they had to deal with, and I had no idea of what they had in mind for me.

I figured they would go back to California. That girl Carol would tell someone, whoever was looking for her friend, that these guys were going to Alaska. But they had California plates, so it was natural for them to go that way. Then they could put the Oregon plates on the car and leave it in a city like Benson said. In a couple of hours from now they could be highballing it past Yreka, Weed, Dunsmuir, and the rest. That was where I wanted to be going, too, but my stomach tightened at the thought of riding with them.

It wasn't just because we were in a stolen car. That was part of it, but the bigger part was the idea I had of that girl stuffed in the trunk. I wanted to be done with these guys. I wished I'd resisted when they told me to drive the car, but I was too dazed then. Now that I had had time to think, I didn't want to be jerked along like a can on a string anymore.

"Well," I said, "maybe I'll just walk from here."

"What do you mean?" Benson's voice had a sharp edge to it.

"If the turn-off is a couple of miles ahead, you can go in and get your stuff and be gone by the time I get there."

"You think you're cuttin' out on us?"

I tried to go easy. I said, "I wouldn't put it that way. I just don't want to go along anymore. You guys go ahead and do what you want. I don't need to know which way you're going."

"Well, you little piss-ant."

Out of the dark I felt the slam of a fist against my left temple, and my feet went out from under me. I forced my eyes open, pushed up onto my hands and knees, and turned towards the car. I felt woozy but I got up, and Benson clobbered me with two more. That time I stayed on the ground. I had all too clear a memory of what he did to that girl and how much remorse he had afterwards.

Floyd stood next to him and said, "Leave him alone. He's just a kid. If he's got any brains at all, he'll keep his mouth shut. Isn't that right, kid?"

"Sure."

Benson took a step forward and stood over me. I could hear the menace in his voice. "Now listen, you little fuck. You don't need to know anything. And remember this. You're in it just as deep as we are. So if anyone ever asks, you don't know a fuckin' thing."

He stood with his fists doubled, and when I didn't answer, he spoke for the last time. His voice was slow and threatening, and he might just as well have been pointing a gun at me. He said, "Don't ever rat on us, kid."

The two of them got into the Chevy, and it pulled away. I was shaky getting back on my feet, and I strained to see the tail lights winking as the car went over a rise in the road.

* * * * *

I made it back to the labor camp in time to get about an hour's worth of sleep. When I went to work I felt ragged and washed-out, but I kept to myself and no one questioned me. I worked there for another week, looking over my shoulder the whole time and flinching whenever someone looked at me. Still no one asked me a word, so whatever Benson and Floyd had said when they left must have been enough.

From Medford I took a bus back to the Sacramento Valley, where the almond harvest was still going on. I got a job picking up windfalls by myself, ahead of the knocking crew. That was near a town named Durham, some thirty miles across the valley from where I had met those guys who were going to make big money. Now I was on my own again, kneeling on the flat, rolled dirt, picking up split-hulled almonds and hearing the shakers rattling like machine guns in the distance.

All the time I was working alone in the heat and the dust, I couldn't quit thinking about the girl named Bev. She came to my mind a hundred times a day, and I kept imagining her stuffed in that trunk full of water.

I knew I was the only person in the world who could do right by her, and I couldn't do it just by hating those other two guys. The decent thing would be to tell someone, but simple fear kept me from doing anything—fear that I would get sent up, fear that I would have to see Floyd and Benson again. So I crawled along, working alone and thinking about what a lousy deal that girl had gotten and what a chump I was to let those guys lord it over me.

Boom-Boom

* * * * *

Almond season came to a close, and I drew my pay. I went back to my cheap hotel room in the town of Chico, a few miles from the orchard, and I holed up there to plan my next move.

I had it in my mind that I needed to put more miles behind me. I thought I could go to the Tulare and Porterville area. Olive season would be starting pretty soon, with oranges after that. I knew some of the towns on the back highway, like Exeter and Strathmore, and I hoped I could go down there and disappear for a while. It wasn't much of a plan, but I felt that I was doing something. It was like the feeling I had when I got back on my feet after having the flu. Life was starting to seem normal. I was still worried, but I wasn't wrapped up in a ball waiting for someone to pound me again.

For the same reason I took the bus down from Medford, I started looking for a car to buy. I didn't want to be on the side of the road hitch-hiking, where any cop who felt like it could stop and question me—or worse, where Floyd and Benson might find me.

I looked in the Chico paper and found a 1953 Plymouth for sale for seventy-five dollars. I called from a pay phone and went to look at it. It had originally been maroon with a white top, but now it had a black right-front fender and a beige-colored hood, plus green spray-spots on the maroon where someone must have done some patching. The right rear door wouldn't stay closed, so it was tied on the inside with a rope that went across to the other door. The car also blew smoke. I got it for sixty dollars.

I made sure all the lights worked, and I got the door welded shut with a couple of spot welds. I didn't want to give a cop any reason to stop me.

After that I went to a surplus store, where I bought a used sleeping bag for three dollars and a lined Levi jacket for five. I felt better equipped now, but I didn't think I had enough travel money, so I went to the employment office.

I went to the window where a clean-cut guy with a Spanish accent had the day-labor jobs. He chewed his gum with his front teeth as he looked at a manila card, and then he asked me if I wanted to work in the vine seed harvest. I didn't know what that was, and he didn't seem to know any more than what the work was called. I said I would take it. A few minutes later I was on my way south to the town of Live Oak.

The referral slip took me to a place south and west of Live Oak. When I got to the field, I found out that vine seed harvest was a polite name for picking up over-ripe cantaloupes. The row boss gave me a metal five-gallon bucket, the kind that tractor grease came in, and put me to work on a row of dying vines.

It was sticky, grubby stoop labor, and noisy as well. Each time I filled my bucket with squishy melons and parts of melons, I took it to a green harvester, which had a hopper, a barrel made of heavy screen, and a loud gas engine. I dumped the bucketful of mush into the hopper, and the barrel turned around and around as it separated the seeds from the pulp. My hands crusted up with juice and dirt, and the fruit flies buzzed around my nose and eyes. But work was work, and I had already understood that this job wasn't going to last long. One of the other workers, a colored man who wore old black dress shoes with no socks, told me we had this field of melons to do, then another of cucumbers, and that would be it.

At five o'clock the labor contractor, a man named Luis, showed up in a Rambler station wagon. The colored man told me they were going to the labor camp, and if I wanted I could ask Luis if he had room.

I said I had a room for one more night so I would see him in the morning. About half a dozen men went with Luis, and that many more left in their own cars. The field boss was still running the machine when I got into my car and headed back to Chico.

Looking back on it, I can see that little by little, I had gotten back into the regular world. I was doing what I knew how, which was to get a job and look after my own details. I still knew that I needed to get gone and disappear, but I wasn't shell-shocked anymore.

I pulled onto Highway 99E, which would take me north through Live Oak, on to Gridley, and from there to Chico. It was a warm, still, hazy afternoon, typical for autumn in the valley. The orchards on either side of the highway had all been harvested, and they had a dry, tired look to them. Some of the leaves were starting to turn yellow. I drove past a big field of pumpkins, and the leaves there were turning pale also. I caught the whiff of a prune dehydrator, which smelled like someone had messed his pants, and then came the dry, sweet-ish aroma of cured alfalfa as I slowed down behind a hay truck.

The truck pulled off in Gridley, so out on the other side of town, past the OK used car lot and the Frostie stand, I had a clear road ahead of me. I stepped on the gas, noted the blue smoke in my mirror, and out of habit looked around for cops.

I was almost at the turnoff for Biggs when I got a hell of a jolt. I was daydreaming like on any other day, thinking about the colored man with no socks and how he had a piece of thin grey cardboard padding the heel of each foot against the inside back part of the shoe. I hadn't seen that before, and I was wondering how common it was. At the same time, I was watching the road ahead of me. A white bread truck was coming my way, and as it loomed on its way past me, I saw a 1956 aqua-and-white Chevy right on its ass.

It was as if my body knew it before I did. I felt a lurch in the pit of my stomach, and I jerked back with my eyes wide open. Fifteen feet away, Bill Benson must have seen me flinch. As he turned to catch a glance at me, his frown turned to a stare of surprise.

A wave of fear rolled through me. Right out of a sunny fall afternoon, the bad dream had come to life. I looked in the side mirror and saw the Chevy's brake lights go on. I stepped on the accelerator, and the Plymouth coughed before it took off. I looked in the mirror again and saw the Chevy turning in the middle of the highway.

There was a turn-off to my right, so I took it. The road was paved, and I thought it might take me to the other highway, the one that went to Oroville. I tromped on the gas.

Up ahead, a flock of chickens had moved into my lane. I slowed down and went around them. When I looked in the rear view, I saw the Chevy turning off the highway. When I looked again, its nose was lifted and it was gaining on me. It scattered the chickens and came straight on.

I thought it was going to ram me in the rear, but instead it pulled up alongside me. Floyd had his window down as I did, and he was hollering at me to pull over. I clamped on the steering wheel with both hands and looked straight ahead. Benson laid onto the horn, and when I didn't pull over, he edged the Chevy close enough that Floyd could have handed me a can of beer, but of course he didn't.

I slammed on the brakes, and the mass of aqua-blue, white, and chrome shot on past me. I turned off the road to my left, stopped, backed up, cranked the wheel again, and headed back to 99E. Behind me as I looked in the mirror, the Chevy was turning around in the middle of the road just as I had done.

I put my foot in the carburetor. As I came up to the spot where the chickens had been, I saw a white one lying dead on the road, and a kid with straight blond hair stared at me as I roared past.

When I got to the stop sign, I decided to turn left to see if I could make it back to Gridley. I had to wait for the traffic to clear, and the Chevy was getting bigger and bigger in my rear view.

I goosed my car out onto the highway, and the Chevy came shooting out behind me. It nearly got broad-sided by a moving van, but it came through clean. In a minute it was right up behind me again, and Benson starting pushing my rear bumper. It made my front wheels turn, and I had to fight to keep the car on the road. I could see Benson scowling in my rear-view mirror, so close he was practically in my back seat. He pointed for me to pull over, but I held the steering wheel as straight as I could.

Up ahead, a livestock truck was stopped in my lane with the left turn signal flashing. I hit the brakes, and the Chevy rammed my rear bumper. I hit the brakes again, then swerved off the highway and headed for a barbed-wire fence that ran along a drainage ditch and ended at the mouth of a culvert. I heard a crunch behind me, and I saw a flash of white and aqua in my side mirror.

The Plymouth came to a rest in the barbed-wire fence, and I saw the heads of Johnson grass sticking up above the front of my hood. I looked back and saw that the Chevy had spun around sideways. Benson was spinning his wheels, but he couldn't get the car to go forward. He put it in reverse, slid it around a few degrees, and tried to go forward again, but the car bucked and would not move. The front left fender was crushed in, and I imagined the metal was jammed against the tire.

I rolled up my window, locked all my doors, and watched as the truck pulled across the highway and parked in a dirt lane. The driver stepped down from the cab with a handful of flares and started setting them out. Cars began to back up as the traffic slowed, and people stared at my car and the other one.

The truck driver crossed the road, came down off the shoulder, and peered in at me. I rolled down the window.

"Are you all right?" he asked. He was a slender fellow with receding blond hair and a small chin.

My mouth was dry and my heart was pounding, but I was glad to talk to someone normal. "Yeah," I said. "I just couldn't get these guys off my ass."

Benson's voice rose up from behind the driver. "You stupid little piss-ant, I just wanted to talk to you. Now look what you've done."

The driver turned and gave him a curious stare. "I think you're the one that ass-ended my truck," he said.

Benson came forward. He waved his hand, and the tips of his fingers came within five feet of me. "This stupid shit wouldn't pull over."

I was still breathing hard, and my voice was shaky as I said, "I've got nothing to say to either of you two." I looked at the driver, hoping that he wouldn't let those guys at me.

"Well, here's the cops," he said. His small chin lifted toward the highway.

A tan sheriff's car had stopped in the middle of the highway with its lights flashing. When the traffic cleared, it made a slow U-turn and came up behind the wrecked Chevy. A deputy with a butch haircut got out and pulled a cap onto his head.

"Is anyone hurt?" he asked.

"It doesn't look like it," said the truck driver.

"What happened?"

"This car here ran into the back of my truck." The driver turned toward me. "Looks like they were chasin' this kid."

The deputy gave a sharp look at Benson. "Is that right? What for?"

"He gave us the finger."

"Do you know him?"

Benson pushed out his lower lip and shook his head. "Never saw him before." Then he gave me an unmistakable look that recalled his words that night in Oregon: *Don't ever rat on us, kid.*

The cop turned to me. "Is that right?"

I hesitated.

"Go ahead and get out of the car," he said.

I had my hands on the steering wheel and didn't let go.

"Come on, get out," said the cop.

I opened the door and stepped out into the weeds. Cars were still crawling by, with people staring. Some of them had their windows rolled down. The evening was warm and heavy, and the smell of sheep drifted on the air. Across the highway, the livestock truck was idling as its signal light flashed.

"Do you know this guy?" asked the deputy. He motioned with his left hand toward Benson.

The truck driver, the cop, and Benson all had their eyes on me. I looked away from them and saw the '56 Chevy with the crunched-up fender and broken headlight. Floyd was leaning against the good fender and smoking a cigarette. I thought of the girl Bev, still in the water-filled trunk of that other car, and my answer seemed to rise with its own strength.

"Yeah," I said. "I know them both."

The deputy's face tightened. "Where from?"

I took a deep breath to steady myself. "From before. I'll tell you all about it."

Hudson

I was standing at the bar in the Crown when a couple at a nearby table waved at me. First the man waved, then the woman.

Half a minute later the man said, "You can come and sit with us if you like. No need to stand there by yourself."

They were a decent-looking couple, clean and well-dressed, somewhere in their middle thirties. I thought they looked familiar, probably from other Friday evenings in the Crown, so I carried my drink over to their table and joined them.

The guy was slender with a narrow face. He had dark hair combed back on both sides and up and over in front, like a carry-over from the Wildroot Cream Oil days. He wore a short-sleeve shirt and a loose necktie. He reminded me of some of the businessmen downtown—not the ones who had been here forever but the ones who came and went, like the manager of the Sprouse-Reitz.

The woman didn't strike me as fitting into any particular class. She didn't look like the type to put on a cap and an apron and start whipping up milkshakes, but she didn't look like the type to drive a new Lincoln with air conditioning, either. She was wearing a sleeveless white blouse and a short yellow skirt, and from what I could see she had a nice figure.

"My name's Nick Pergamino," the guy said. "And this is my wife, Carolyn."

"I'm Tommy Hudson."

"Like the car, huh?"

"That's right," I said.

"What do you do?"

"Field work. Right now I'm a row boss in the peaches."

"Good for you."

"What about yourself?"

"I sell insurance. Do you own your own home?"

"No," I said. "I rent."

"I sell car insurance, too."

"I should probably get some."

"Everyone should have it. Too many people go without it."

"I know," I said, with a little twinge of guilt. "It's the cost, you know."

"Are you thirty yet?"

"No, I'm a few years short of it."

"Even at that, I can get you a better rate than you might think."

I glanced at his wife, Carolyn. She had friendly blue eyes and shiny, bleach-blond hair that flipped up in a curl above her shoulders. I took her for a few years younger than her husband. "What do you think?" I asked. "Will he get me a deal?"

"Probably," she answered. "Lots of people say they get better rates with him than anyone else."

Nick looked up and spoke in a loud voice. "Hey, Marcie. Get us a round here, would you?"

Marcie turned and stood by our table. Her dark hair was combed out into a mound and sprayed in place, and her long eyelashes were shiny. Her full breasts rode high in a white blouse. She looked at each of us as she spoke. "Seven-and-seven, Tom Collins. Bourbon and water for you, Tommy?"

"Sure." I met her dark eyes, then watched her as she walked away, a nice firm figure in a black skirt.

"So you're a row boss," Nick said. "How long does the season last?"

"About six weeks. The place where I work tries to be done by Labor Day."

"Then you stay on with them, or you go to work for someone else?"

"I usually find work in the almonds about then. When the high school and college kids go back to school, there's work to be found. A little later I go to work row-bossin' in the olives and then the oranges."

"How far do you drive every day?"

"Usually no more than twenty miles each way."

"See, that's not so much. I bet I can get you a rate you wouldn't believe. What do you drive?"

"A '55 Dodge."

"Oh, hell. I can fix you up. You're crazy not to be insured. All it takes is one telephone pole."

"I know."

He looked up and smiled. "Hey, Marcie. By golly, you're a good girl. See what you brought us." He creased a five-dollar bill and laid it on her tray. "Keep the change."

"Well, thanks, Nick."

"You betcha."

I thought his eyes lingered on her a little longer than they should when his wife was sitting right there. I turned to Carolyn and said, "How long have you folks lived in town?"

"Less than a year."

"I thought I'd seen you before. Probably in here."

"You look familiar, too." She smiled.

Nick came back into the conversation. "Do you ski, Tommy?"

"Water ski? No, not really."

"I've got a friend who's got a boat. He's always tryin' to get us to go out. Said we could invite someone."

"I don't know," I said.

"Oh, you don't have to ski. Carolyn doesn't. You could just go along and drink beer. We could invite you and Marcie."

"That's Nick's angle," said Carolyn. She turned to her husband. "You don't know if he even knows Marcie, much less whether he likes her."

Nick rattled the ice in the drink he was finishing. "Well, do you know her?"

"Sure. I think she's swell."

"Maybe we'll ask her, then. Drink up." He nodded at my glass.

"I don't get much time off this time of year," I said. "A lot of these crops go seven days a week."

"Oh, we don't have to do it tomorrow." Nick lifted a pack of L&M's from the table and shook one out. He flipped open a heavy Ronson, lit his cigarette, and snapped the lighter shut. "I should have asked. You're not married, are you?"

"Oh, no. I'd get a better rate if I was, though, wouldn't I?"

"Huh? Oh, yeah. Married, over thirty. You'd make a killin'."

"Somethin' to look forward to."

Nick blew out a stream of smoke. "We'll fix you up."

We drank more than we should have, or at least I did. I tried to pay my share, but Nick kept ordering drinks. After about three hours I was buzzed, and Nick was being every-one's friend. For a while he sat at a table with another couple, and Carolyn and I were left at ours.

"Nick's that way," she said. "Wants everyone to go to his party. Don't let him make you do anything you don't want."

"Oh, I won't." I looked at my drink and then at her. "I hate to leave, but I've got to work tomorrow."

She smiled at me. It was one of those clear moments in the middle of a hazy night at the bar. "It's nice meeting you," she said. "We'll get together again."

"Sure." I put two dollars on the table for a tip, waved to Nick, and called out a good-night to Marcie. She raised her hand up to shoulder level in a fluttering wave, then leaned to one side to take a customer's order. The noise of the bar faded as I walked out into the warm night and headed for my car. The streetlight on the corner was buzzing, and a toad had come out to catch the bugs where they fell on the sidewalk.

* * * * *

We finished the orchard a little before noon on Wednesday, and we weren't going to start the next one until the following morning, so when we got the ladders and buckets moved I asked for the rest of the afternoon off.

The owner, Milt, asked me what I needed to do.

I told him I wanted to get a haircut and take some shoes to get them re-soled.

He looked at my feet.

"Not these," I said. "Another pair. It's just that I never have time off when the shoe shop's open."

"I guess," he said.

The day was heating up as I drove into town. I decided to take care of the shoes first and not be impatient if I had to wait in the barber shop.

I left off the shoes in a little hole-in-the-wall place around the corner from the barber's. The corner itself was taken up by Calvin's Dairy Fountain. I never knew if Calvin was a first or last name. Men a little younger than my father were named Calvin, which I didn't think much about until I read an obituary of one who had died early, in a car wreck, and his middle name was Coolidge. If someone from that generation had put up the sign on the corner fountain, he would have had to have done it at an early age, because it was an old-style sign from the forties, ridged and pale green with white letters. Inside, the stools along the counter had pale green seats, and the large rectangular sign with the list of cones and shakes had a frame painted in the same color.

As I walked past the window, I glanced in. A group of businessmen, all in short-sleeve white shirts, sat around a table. They had tall soda glasses in front of them, and they looked like a casual, comfortable bunch. I recognized a jeweler and a used-car salesman. Nick Pergamino, the insurance agent, was paying attention to a man who had brown hair cut in a flat top. The man looked like George Jones, and I thought I had seen him on some earlier occasion setting up bicycles in the window of the Western Auto store.

I took a seat in the barber shop. An old, heavy-set man was getting his hair cut, and a kid about sixteen was sitting in a chair reading a sports magazine. The old man had an Irish accent and was telling how they skinned sheep in the old country. I figured I was in for a long wait, so I picked up the newspaper for a daily dose of anti-Communist news reporting.

The barber finished with the old man, who stood up and paid for his haircut. The kid put aside his magazine, took a hat off the rack, and handed it to the old man. The two of them went out into the glaring afternoon and paused on the sidewalk as the old man gave the kid a quarter. Then they disappeared in the direction of Calvin's Dairy Fountain.

The barber set his broom and long-handled dust pan in the corner and swung the chair around. "Next."

As I took a seat in the swivel chair, I saw the old man walking across the street toward the Pastime Club, which sat on the corner west of the dairy fountain.

The barber went right into his chatter, trying me out on one topic and another until he settled on deer hunting. He opened a wooden drawer and showed me the center part he had torn out of a bull's eye target. It had three little holes close together in the smallest circle.

"You could cover that group with a half-dollar," he said.

"Sure could."

"I shot these just last week."

"That's good."

He talked on, telling me about deer he had shot, deer he had missed, a rainstorm that had soaked his rifle stock, and a rivet that had fallen out of his sling and had caused him to drop his rifle. I was wondering how much smaller the details would get when he loosened the cape and swirled it away like a bullfighter.

"All done."

I gave him two dollars, and as he handed me the quarter in change, I waved and said, "Keep it."

"Thanks," he said. "I hope you get a deer."

"Same to you."

I walked out into the hot, bright afternoon. I had left my straw hat in my car, so I could feel the sun on my ears and neck as I walked north toward the dairy fountain. Just before I reached the corner, I saw movement at the front door of the Pastime. It lay on the shady side of the street, so I didn't make out the person right away. Then I saw that it was the old man who had gotten his hair cut. He stood in the shade, smoking a cigar. A bell tinkled, and the door on my right opened. I stopped, thinking it might be Nick Pergamino, but it was the kid who had been in the barber shop. I figured his grandfather had given him the two bits to have a Coke while the old man drank a beer in the saloon. I nodded to the kid and let him go past me.

Around the corner, I walked along a sliver of shade until I came to my car. As I stepped off the curb and waited at the left rear fender, a beige-colored '64 Buick came to a stop in front of me. The electric window on the passenger's side rolled down, and a woman in light colors looked out from the red interior.

"Hey, stranger."

My interest perked up. It was Carolyn Pergamino, look-ing trim and fresh. "Well, hello," I said. "What are you up to?"

"Nothin' much." She looked in her rear-view mirror. "Are you comin' to happy hour this Friday?"

"I might."

"Why don't you?" She glanced at the mirror again and said, "I've got to go. See you later."

"Sure." I watched the Buick pull away. She looked at me in the rear-view and waved, so I waved back.

* * * * *

I didn't get away from the orchard until after six on Friday, so happy hour was well over by the time I got cleaned up and made it to the Crown. Nick and Carolyn were still there, sit-ting at a table with a couple I thought I recognized from the week before.

Nick waved me over and told me to sit down. When I did, he introduced me to Don and Shirley. Don had his own pitcher of beer, and Shirley sat looking at a tall, pink, slushy-looking drink with two straws sticking out of it. Nick went on to say that Don was a parts salesman. He worked for a distributor. Fan belts, air cleaners, gaskets, you name it.

"And Shirley, she's just Shirley."

"What else would she be?" asked Carolyn.

"Shirley You Jest. Ha-ha-ha."

Shirley forced a smile, and Don drank from his glass of beer.

Carolyn spoke to me. "Been workin' hard?"

"Pretty long hours."

"Don't kid me," Nick said. "I saw you downtown in the middle of the day, what, day before yesterday."

"Well, we got done early, so I took a couple of hours off to run errands."

"Yeah, I saw you in the barber shop. Hey, here's Marcie." He raised his head and smiled. "Let's have some drinks, hon. One for Tommy. Bourbon and water, right? And one for me. You, Carolyn? Okay. Just me and Tommy."

Marcie was in her regular outfit, a white blouse and a black skirt. Her dark hair glistened.

I caught her eye. "Hi, Marcie."

"Hi."

I made myself not watch her as she walked away, but I saw that Nick wasn't quite so disciplined. I caught a glance from Carolyn, one of those flickers that said we understood each other for the moment.

The drinks came, and Nick laid a creased ten-dollar bill on her tray. With his usual smile he said, "That's our girl."

Don was no slouch at putting away the beer, but Shirley didn't touch her drink. She sat straight up in her chair with her hands in her lap. She had a puffy hairdo and a puffy face, and it seemed to me that she did not like Nick.

Don was telling a story about another salesman who was a kiss-ass and was trying to cut in on his territory. Nick said if it was him, he would tell the guy about it. Don said it wasn't an easy thing to do, the way things were.

"So if the foo shits, you have to wear it?"

"You find a way around it." Don poured the last of the pitcher into his glass.

Nick raised his head and looked around. "We'll get you another one. Where's Marcie?"

Shirley turned her bouffant head and frowned at her husband.

Don held up his hand. "This is all for me, Nick. Thanks."

A few minutes later, Don and Shirley were gone. Marcie picked up the empty pitcher and beer glass and the tall, full glass of cloudy pink stuff.

Nick smiled. "Do you drink those things, Marcie?"

"No, not me."

"What do you drink?"

"It all depends."

"Same here. I can drink a lot of things, but not those." As Marcie walked away, Nick said to me, "Even if it is titty pink."

I stayed long enough to buy Nick and Carolyn a drink, and then I called it quits. As I stood up and said good-night, I caught that look again from Carolyn, the quick glance that said we shared some kind of understanding. I looked for Marcie, said good-night to her, and walked out into the warm night. A few sounds carried on the air—a car from a couple of blocks away, music and voices drifting out of the open door of the No-Tell. The toad had not yet showed up beneath the street light, but there were a few bugs lying on their backs, kicking their legs, and waiting for him.

* * * * *

I came out of the grocery store on Monday evening and found Carolyn in her beige Buick parked next to my car. I went around to her window.

Her face was drawn a little tight, but she smiled as she said, "Hi, there."

"Hi. What's up?"

"Not much. I saw your car, so I thought I'd pull in and say hi."

"Nice of you." From where I stood I could see her short skirt. I looked up and away, then came back to meet her eyes. "Are you shopping, too, or just driving around?"

"I did my shopping earlier."

I could feel my heartbeat picking up. "Well, it's nice to see you."

"It sure is." She held me with her eyes. "Do you think I could talk to you?"

I shrugged. "I guess so. Where's Nick?"

"He plays poker on Mondays."

"Oh." I looked around again. "Do you want to go some place and have a cup of coffee?"

She stared ahead for a couple of seconds until she came back to me. "Could we go to your place? I'd just as soon not be seen."

My eyes widened, and my mouth felt dry. "I suppose we could. Do you know where I live?"

"In that old four-plex by the tracks, don't you?"

"That's right." I frowned at her car. "Are you going to leave this out front?"

"I know where I can park."

"Okay. Give me a few minutes' head start, and I'll answer the door as soon as you knock. Better yet, I'll leave it open. Mine's number four."

I was fidgety as hell as I drove home and went into my apartment. I put my groceries away and was straightening up a couple of things when I heard the rap of fingernails on the door. I opened it further, and she walked in.

I had to catch my breath. She looked trim as always, in her sleeveless blouse and short skirt, and she had a serious look about her.

"I don't have much to offer," I said. "I didn't think to stop and get something."

"That's okay."

"All I've got is a couple of cans of beer."

"I'll drink a beer."

I went to the kitchen, took out the two cans of Coors, and opened them. When I came back into the living room, she was standing in front of a picture on the wall. As I handed her the beer I said, "That's a Hudson."

"Oh, yeah. I remember now."

"It's a 1951. I got it off a calendar. My old man had one, same year model, black and shiny just like that one."

"When you were little?"

"Yeah. My old man had cattle. Bought and sold 'em, and he drove that Hudson to auction yards all the way from Klamath Falls to L.A. He wore a black Stetson. My brother and I did, too. We were about six and seven. That's how I remember the Hudson, the three of us goin' down the highway in our black hats. My old man could run that car up to a hundred, but a lot of the time he kept it at eighty. He'd slow down when he came up behind a car, and my brother and I would say, 'Pass him, Daddy. Pass him.' And he would."

Carolyn smiled. "I can just see you, like a little cowboy."

"That's what we were, until he went broke. After that it was workin' for wages. He always wanted to get back into business, but he never did."

"Is he—?"

"He died a few years ago."

"And your brother?"

"He's still alive. He's a year younger than I am. I see him once in a while."

"That's good."

I raised my beer and took a drink. She did the same, then took another look at the picture.

"Shall we sit down?" I said.

"Sure." She moved to the couch. "You can sit here, too, so we don't have to shout."

I took a deep breath and sat down. "Do you need an ash tray?"

"No, not now."

I drank from my beer. Just the taste of it settled my nerves a little.

"Workin' long hours?" she said.

"In spite of what some people say. And it's been a while since I've had a day off."

"You seem like you're pretty responsible."

"I've got a job, and I do my work."

She gave me a smile. "Are you the kind of boy that's all work and no play?"

"I wouldn't say that."

She had one leg hiked over the other, and she gave it a swing. "What do you like to play?"

Things were going faster than I expected, but I didn't want to get left behind. So I said, "I think girls know what boys like. We get accused of it all the time."

"Now that's a boy, for sure." She took a drink and set the can on the end table. Then she held out her hand, nodded at my beer, and said, "Here, give me yours."

I leaned forward, handed her the can, and waited until she set it next to hers. Then I moved toward her.

When the distance between us was gone, I felt a huge rush. In no time at all, I was kissing her all over her upper body. Then we stood up, and I waltzed her to the bedroom. I undressed her, shucked my own clothes in an instant, and went on. I did everything I knew, uptown and downtown, and then we were doing it the good old-fashioned way, with her on her back, moving her hips up and down, drawing me in like I had never felt before, pulling me out of myself and into a dark canyon of ecstasy as I lost sense of everything but the sensation.

I lay on my side, trying to catch my breath. "Boy, that was something," I said. "I don't know if I've ever had it that intense before."

"It was good." She played her fingers on my ribs.

"Do you want an ashtray now?"

"I don't smoke much at all."

"I'll go get our beers."

After we had a drink, I couldn't stay away from her. I went back to kissing every bit of her body as she lay on her back, and her response was almost electrical. In a while I was ready to go again, and like the first time, I was lost in the plunge.

Now we were both calm. I pulled down the bedclothes, and we covered ourselves with a sheet.

"It's quiet here," she said.

"Right now it is. Sometimes they park a locomotive out there and it idles for two or three days at a time."

"Really? That must be aggravating."

"You get used to it."

Her eyes played over my face, and she smiled.

"Is there something funny?" I asked.

"I'm imagining you as a little cowboy in a black hat."

"Well, those days are gone, I'm afraid."

"But you've still got it in you."

"Oh, I suppose. All the time I was growing up, my old man said we would get it back. My brother and I would be able to grow up like he did, with a gun and a horse and a place of our own. But we didn't. And I'm still working for wages."

"And you don't think you'll ever get it back?"

"Not like my old man had it. Those days are past, when a guy could go out, work hard, save up, and get his own place. It all costs too much now—land, cattle, trucks. I'd be lucky to rent a few acres and raise a few head of calves."

"Oh, you'll do fine."

"I hope I do something." I ran the back of my finger along her ribs. "But you didn't come here to listen to all of this."

"It's all right."

"I'm sure glad you came, though. When I saw you there in front of the store, I didn't know what you wanted to talk about. But this turned out great."

She didn't say anything. She seemed to be studying me.

"Was there something in particular, then?" I asked.

"Well, there was. I didn't actually have this other part planned. It just kind of happened."

"Happened in a pretty good way."

"Oh, yeah."

Her answer sounded short, so I said, "Go ahead and tell me the other part."

She took a steady breath and said, "It's about Marcie."

Oh, shit, I thought. *Nick has hooked up with Marcie, and that's what this is about. Getting even.*

Carolyn said, "I didn't know if you heard."

"No, I haven't heard anything."

"They found her dead."

Everything seemed to drop, and time seemed to stand still. "When did that happen?"

"This morning. She'd been there since some time over the weekend."

I felt as I'd had the wind knocked out of me. "Any idea how it happened? I mean, did someone—?"

Carolyn nodded her head. "Someone did it."

"Do they have any idea of who it might have been?"

She moved her head back and forth. "The last time we saw her was Friday night. I know the first thing you would think of would be Nick."

"Oh, no," I said, which I knew was a lie.

"We went home together on Friday night, and he didn't go anywhere by himself for the rest of the weekend."

"Does he sometimes?"

"Oh, he's a real slummer. But he didn't this time, unless it was when I was dead asleep. Which I don't think happened."

I let out another long, tired breath. "Jesus, this is hard to believe."

"Isn't it, though?" Carolyn focused her eyes on me. "Do you have any ideas on it?"

"Me? No, I don't know her that well. Not that I would have minded, but I never got that far along with her." I frowned. "What does Nick say?"

"I've barely talked to him. The news just got around to-day, and he went to play poker not too long after work. They drink beer and eat ham-and-cheese sandwiches on poker night. It's part of their ritual."

"Sure." A shadow of worry crossed my mind. "You don't think he'd be out looking for you right now, do you?"

"No, not on poker night."

"Is he pretty stuck on playing cards?"

"No, but he wouldn't want anyone to think he didn't have everything under control."

"How late does he stay out?"

"Usually till about midnight. I'll be home way before that."

I thought we might have time for one more, and I was right.

* * * * *

All the next day as I trudged through the orchard, seeing that the workers didn't pick too many green peaches or leave too many ripe ones, I had a couple of thoughts that kept coming back. One was a vague idea of Marcie being found dead in her apartment, and the other was of me tumbling headlong into oblivion with Carolyn. The images played back and forth, like agony and ecstasy, as I had heard it put. And with both scenarios came the question of why.

In Marcie's case, I had no answer at all. I couldn't imagine anyone having a reason to do anything to her—except for the reasons people have to begin with and find someone to take them out on.

With Carolyn, I had too many answers, and none that held up strong enough. I could tell myself she came to see me because she found me handsome and irresistible, but I was sure that was not the whole story. The same went for the idea that she was getting even with Nick or getting away with something. She did take pleasure in the act itself, and I had to admit she was better at it than women I had known who did it for a living, but I didn't think that was the whole story, either. She had started by saying she wanted to talk to me, so maybe it was a way she had of talking on a certain level, when all the barriers were gone. Aside from the sex act, the only thing we had in common was her husband, but I doubted she would go to that length just to tell me her husband was a slummer but she didn't think he was guilty of anything with Marcie.

And so I went round and round on these questions and always came back to nothing—nothing, that is, except the knowledge that I wanted to take that plunge again.

Meanwhile I walked the rows of peach trees, making sure the pickers kept to their own trees, didn't pick someone else's bottoms, didn't skip any trees, and didn't pull any other stunts. I kept track of who picked which trees, who filled which bins, and who was ready to move to the next set or row. I kept Larry, the forklift driver, busy hauling out full bins and moving partial ones.

A couple of the pickers asked me if I had heard about the barmaid who was killed, and I said I didn't know anything about it. The pickers weren't from here anyway, so it was just an item of curiosity to them. Larry had more interest in it, not because he knew Marcie but because he had a girlfriend who wanted to wait tables in a bar and he was dead-set against it. So the story for him was one good reason that strengthened his side of an argument.

Marcie's funeral came and went. I didn't know her well enough to ask for time off. I did remember her, though, and at two o'clock on Friday afternoon, when her friends and family would be gathering at the funeral home, I went to the edge of the orchard and gazed down the road that led towards town. I said a few words to myself, then walked back in among the trees.

A wave of emptiness washed through me, and I stood for a moment with my hand resting on a branch about as big around as my arm. I took a deep breath to steady myself, then turned at the sound of something on the road. A flatbed truck loaded with hay bales went rumbling by, and then, from the opposite direction, coming from town, a beige-colored car rolled along at about fifty miles an hour. I held still. As it came closer I saw that it was a Buick, and then I saw Nick Pergamino behind the wheel. He was wearing sunglasses, and he looked relaxed. His hands were out of sight, so I imagined he held the steering wheel at the bottom. He didn't look to either side as he cruised by, and for all any bystander could tell, he was driving out to the country to buy a jar of honey or a dozen eggs.

* * * * *

On Friday as well as the rest of the weekend I stayed away from all of the bars in town. I didn't want to hear anyone talking about Marcie in any way, and I didn't want to run into Nick Pergamino.

As for Carolyn, we had left it open that she might call me on the next available Monday. After making it through the weekend, I started getting antsy. I kept looking at my watch all afternoon on Monday, and I took a shower as soon as I got home. I ate a quick dinner of reheated macaroni and was cleaning up the kitchen when the phone rang.

"Hello, Tommy?"

"Hi, there. Glad to hear from you." I felt a relief at hearing her voice, but the other tension was still there.

"Are you going to be home?"

"I don't plan to go anywhere."

"Would it be all right if I came over?"

A flutter went through me. "More than all right."

"Okay. I'll be there in a little bit."

This time I locked the door behind her as soon as she came in, and we went straight to the bedroom. We nearly devoured each other, and then I fell into the deep, dark canyon with waves of nothingness folding over me. A little while later I came to the surface and lay on my side, as if I had been washed ashore.

"Whew. That was something," I said. "Incredible."

"Expialidocious," she said, with a laugh.

"I've got to catch my breath."

"Go ahead."

She was looking at me again as she had on the earlier occasion.

"Do you still see me as the little cowboy in the black hat?"

"I was thinking of something you said last time."

"What was that?"

"The part about guns and horses."

"Oh, yeah."

"They seemed like, so much a part of what you were talking about."

"I guess so. They were the things my old man had when he was growing up and that he still had when he was in business. But he had to sell his horses, and his saddles. He sold some of his guns, then pawned the others from time to time until he either lost them or sold them, too."

"What kind of guns?"

"Oh, hunting rifles, like for deer, and then your average .22 and shotgun."

"Are those for hunting, too?"

"Pretty much. That, and target practice."

"And that was some of what you wanted to get back to, the hunting?"

"Uh-huh. There was something there, part of a way of life, I guess, that was above low class. But we didn't get it back, not when he was alive. And then my brother got into trouble, and he can't have guns anymore."

"Do you?"

"I've worked my way up. I have a deer rifle." I thought of telling her about my brother's .357, but I didn't.

"So you hunt."

"When I can. That's why I hope we finish peach season by Labor Day."

"Well, I've never been around it. Hunting."

"I have. A little bit. I should have learned from my old man, but it was in the past by then. So I learned from others. It didn't start out well."

"Oh, really?"

I was relaxed now, and in no hurry. "Yeah," I said. "I was out on my own, not too long after high school. I was workin' over by Gridley, about fifty miles from here. There was a government camp where I stayed for a while, and this other guy said he knew how to get a deer. He invited a girl, so that made it more interesting. But all he had was a pistol. I thought, he's not going to get very much with that. You know, a pistol doesn't have much range."

"Right."

"So we go out to this bean field, and it's night time. He's got a spotlight he made out of a car headlight and a round oat-meal box. He hooks the headlight up to some wires that he connects under the dash, and he's got a jacklight. But there's no deer. He has me hold the light, and he gets out to show the girl how to shoot the gun. Puts his arms around her to help her hold the gun. All that, you know."

"Sure."

"Then we drive around a little, and still we don't see any deer. So we head back to the camp, and out on a country road we see a car pulled off and pointed into an orchard. He gets the car in his headlights, then gets out and shoots the hell out of the back window, and it shatters in a million pieces. But it turns out there's a couple in the back seat, and they come bailin' out with no clothes on."

"Oh, my God."

"Oh, yeah. Hell of a mess. We got out of there. When we got back to the camp he sort of threatened me, told me that if anyone asked, I had to say we were in the camp the whole time. I didn't know about that because any number of people could have seen us leave. But in the end it didn't matter. A couple of guys caught up with him one night, ran him off the road, and beat him within an inch of his life."

"That's one way to learn not to mess around with guns."

"You'd think so."

"But that wasn't really hunting."

"No, it wasn't. After that I went around with a guy I knew from high school, but he was just a road-hunter. He shot everything from the cab, and if things didn't look good, like he could be seen too easily dragging a deer off someone's property, he'd just leave it."

"That doesn't sound very sporting."

"It isn't. So after a couple of seasons with him, I found someone else to go with. He was an older guy, almost as old as my old man. We worked together building fence, and he invited me to go along with him. I got my head a little straighter about hunting after that."

"Well, that's good. Do you have much success at it?"

"Not as much as I'd like, but I'm still learning." I thought for a second. "You seem kind of interested in all this."

"Like I said, I've never been around it. Hunting always seemed like one of those things that some people did and some people didn't. Actually, horses were that way, too. People who had them seemed a little different."

"I know what you mean. My old man talked about those things, but we didn't have 'em. They belonged to that other life."

"But you hunt now. You say you have a deer rifle. Do you think you'll have a horse?"

"Oh, that's a ways off yet, if at all. Like owning my own place. It's something I hope to do, but I have to get there first. Working your way up is not easy."

"You're tellin' me. We can barely pay for the car we drive."

"I thought insurance agents had it easy."

"Maybe some of them do. But we've been together seven years, and we've lived in four towns. Every time we move, it takes about two years to pay it off."

"No kids?"

"Nick says we need to wait till we can afford it. I think he wants to avoid the responsibility."

"Do you think you'll have kids?"

"I hope so. I just don't know when."

I rolled over towards her. "As long as you don't forget how."

"It's a reason to stay in practice." She took me to her, and I was lost again.

I had had the foresight to buy a six-pack of beer, so when we were in a calm afterwards, I brought us each a can of Coors. She sat up in bed with the sheet across her lap as I handed her a beer. I climbed in to sit beside her.

"I was hoping you could come by," I said.

"I don't know that I'll always be able to."

John D. Nesbitt

"Enjoy the moment."

She smiled. "That's what I say."

I took a drink. "You know, I thought about you all week. I just couldn't wait to be with you again. But I have to tell myself that at some point it might have to end, just like that."

"Better not to think about it."

I took a couple of seconds to phrase my question. "Do you think he'd do something—?"

"Violent?"

"Well, yeah."

"I don't know. I think he might be capable."

"Really? Violent with me, with you—?"

"Either one. Maybe me more than you. I think he's capable of being violent with a woman."

Something clicked. "But you don't think he had anything to do with Marcie."

"I never said I thought he wasn't capable. I just said I didn't think he left the house."

"But he could have done something like that?"

She shrugged. "Possibly."

I gave her a close look. "Has he ever been rough with you?"

She frowned and she tipped her head, but she didn't say anything.

"Maybe it's not any of my business, but—"

"Yes, he has," she said. "But not for a while." She paused as she took a drink of beer. "You see, he liked to play a little rough. When we were having sex, he got where he liked to choke me. It was something he picked up somewhere. He

192

said it was real exciting for the woman, but it sure wasn't for me. I told him I didn't want to, and he said okay, but then when we'd get into it, he'd try it again. So finally I put a stop to the whole thing."

"You mean you–"

"Yeah. I cut him off. He doesn't come into my room, and I don't go into his."

Sheesh, I thought. *What a loss on his part.* But I said, "So if you don't sleep in the same room, you don't know for sure whether he comes or goes."

"I think I usually do, but I can't be dead certain."

I lay still for a long moment. Even if she wasn't sleeping with him at the present, I thought I was way too close for comfort. And here I'd been chattering on about guns this and guns that. I gave her another close look. "Do you think he did it, then?"

"Marcie? I think he could have."

I let it sink in a little more. "You know, this is the kind of thing you ought to tell someone else."

"You mean the police."

"Well, yeah."

"I've thought of it, of course. But if I'm not right, or even if I am and they don't do anything, I'm afraid of what he'd do to me."

"And so you tell me instead. If he finds out about us, and if he's got anything to keep secret, I mean, he could come unglued."

"I thought you were a safe person to tell."

It occurred to me that the barriers had been knocked down well enough for me to be told these kinds of things. "I guess in some ways I am. But if I thought he really did it, I don't know if I could just sit by. After all, I knew Marcie. She's not just someone down in Sacramento that you hear about on the news." I paused. "Or is that why you told me? Thinking maybe I would say something? Is that why I'm safe?"

She gave a shrug. "I don't know. You just seem so . . . capable."

"Like, once you told me, I would know what to do?"

She smiled and nodded. "Something like that." She laid her hand on the back of my neck. It was a light touch, but along with her words, it ran a current through me. "You always know what to do."

Don't waste the opportunity, I thought. I had that much presence of mind, plus the knowledge that she was estranged in a way from her husband, which made things seem more justified. But after a few clear seconds I was pulled in as deep as ever and lost my sense of everything but the pure sensation, and it was not until later, much later, after she had put on her clothes and gone home, that I wondered again why she had told me what she did about her husband, and whether it had anything to do with her interest in what kinds of guns I had. As I put it in simple terms to myself, maybe she thought I could take care of myself if the guy got out of hand.

* * * * *

The picking crew moved on to another orchard, across the

county road and west about half a mile. Two or three times a day I would end up at the edge of the orchard and look up and down the road. Most of the time I saw nothing, but maybe once a day I would see a car or truck coming, never very fast. I saw the same hay truck twice, an early 1950's Chevrolet with a dull, dark green cab and a suicide knob at the top of the steering wheel. It had a similar load each time, five tiers of two-wire bales, and the alfalfa smell came drifting toward me as I stood inside the orchard.

I expected to see Nick Pergamino again, for the same reason that whenever I saw a rooster pheasant or a buck deer in a particular place, I always expected to see one there again. But I did not see Nick Pergamino again on County Road 44.

In proportion to the rest of the day, I spent very little time looking down the road. Most of the time I was checking on the pickers, keeping the crew organized, and keeping track of who picked what. During all that, Carolyn drifted through my mind a thousand times a day. I wondered how long our affair would last, whether she would ever split up with her husband, what she expected out of me, and whether she would ditch me as soon as things got difficult. I thought also of the things we had talked about and the specific things we had done. Always I felt a pull, a deep desire to shed everything and merge again, lose myself in the pleasure that had no borders. I would not have thought I could be hooked by something like that, and I did not have an awareness that I was, but the fall into the dark canyon was by far what I thought about the most.

* * * * *

The phone rang on Monday, and I felt a huge relief when I heard a cheery tone to her voice.

"Hi, there, stranger. Have you got time to visit?"

"You mean on the phone?"

"No, I mean time *for* a visit."

"Oh, you mean here." My heartbeat picked up, and I felt a small rush of excitement.

She laughed. "I could spell it out."

"That would take too long. By all means, come on over."

I had her in my arms and was locking the door at the same time. I kissed her up and down and all over, undressed her halfway in the living room, carried her to the bedroom, finished with her undressing, buried my face in her perky bosom and her golden fleece, felt her total release as she gave herself to me, then lost all sense of my own boundaries as I was pulled into her warm, moist, pulsing center.

She must have hungered for it as much as I did, for we hardly caught our breath after the first go-around before we went into it again. She was steady and vigorous, and we came out even at the end.

She had a glow of contentment as we lay on our sides looking at each other. "It's like the old joke," she said. "This guy and girl are always going at it like that, and he says, 'We got to slow down. Just do it once a night. All night long.' And the girl says, 'We could do it even better. Just once a week.'"

I laughed. "Boy, you'd think you'd get to where it was routine at some point, but it's always new."

"Did you miss me?"

"It wasn't a gun in my pocket."

"I guess not." She winked and said, "How 'bout it, sailor? Buy me a drink?"

"It so happens I have some on hand."

I fetched two cans of beer, and we sat up in bed and drank them like before.

"So tell me," I said. "What's new?"

"Not much. How about you?"

I shrugged. "I don't know. I've thought about what you said last time, about a certain party's tendency to do things kind of rough."

"Uh-huh."

"And from what I've heard, from this fellow who drives forklift, that's how Marcie was done in."

"Choked."

"Um, yeah."

"I know. I heard the same thing at the beauty shop. Actually, I had heard it before I talked to you last time, but I didn't quite get around to mentioning it."

"Makes it seem more likely, or at least possible, doesn't it?"

She didn't answer.

"Did I go too far?" I asked.

"Oh, no. I just don't know how much to say myself."

"Well, don't worry about me. Say what you think you want to. As far as I'm concerned, there's no reason to hold things back from one another. I mean, that's one thing about an affair, isn't it? You're supposed to have a level of confidence that you wouldn't have with your regular partner?"

"I don't know. I mean, about how much I want to say."

"Well, that's okay, too." I drank from my beer. "You don't want to be in a position where you say something and then wish you hadn't."

"Oh, to hell with it. If this ever comes back on me, it won't be through you."

"You can count on that."

She was quiet for a few seconds and then said, "Okay. It goes like this. When we first got married, we lived in Bakersfield. After a couple of years we moved to Merced, and a couple of years after that we moved to Turlock. From there we came here. Each time, it was supposed to be a better town and a better opportunity. But it never was. If anything, things got a little poorer each time. Mostly a matter of fewer customers, I think. Or clients."

"So is he one of those guys who always has to be on the move, always changing things?"

"To tell you the truth, I don't know him well enough to answer that. But what all three of those towns had in common was that before we left each time, a girl got killed. They were always lower-class girls, like Marcie."

I must have flinched, because she held up her hand.

"I don't mean Marcie was low-class by nature, but she had a job that was, well, not really high up. That's the way these other girls were. Two of them worked in bars, and one of them was like a street girl."

"And they all died the same way?"

"They were all choked, and they were all left spread-eagled on the bed, with no clothes on."

"Marcie too?"

"As I heard it."

I pulled in a slow, deep breath. "That's quite a bit," I said. "If it's true, it's got to be more than just coincidence."

"It's true. I read it in the papers. Each time. Someone could find those back issues, and it's all there. Not to mention in the police reports."

I exhaled. "And you've had kind of an inkling of this as you went along?"

"Kind of. You know, you prefer not to think about it. But it stays with you, and it grows."

We finished our beer and decided to take a shower. She was not very shy about her body, so she let me wash her all over. I used a lot of suds, and she was clean as could be when we shut off the water. Then I took a towel and dried her everywhere I had washed her.

By now we were in the mood again, and she didn't seem to worry about doing it right after she had gotten clean. I didn't worry either, but as she would say, I was a boy.

* * * * *

Peach season came to a close on a Sunday afternoon, almost a week before the Labor Day weekend. We finished the orchard in a rush, and the pickers waited in the shade of the trees near their cars as I made the final tallies, checked my count against Larry the forklift driver's, and gave the sheets and tickets to Milt the owner. Larry and I hauled the ladders and buckets to the barn, and when we got back, Milt was making out the last checks for the pickers. When he was done with them, he gave Larry and me each an envelope.

Mine had two blue-green checks in it, one that paid me through Sunday and one that was a hundred-dollar bonus for the whole harvest. From the look on Larry's face, I figured he had fared just as well. We shook hands all the way around, and that was the end of peach season.

Back in town, the envelope with the two checks rested on the kitchen table as I sat in my chair in front of the swamp cooler. For as much as I wanted to, I couldn't relax. One part of me wanted to have a few drinks, sleep in late, get my things together the next day, and go deer hunting. The part of me that was running things, though, the restless part, wanted to find out if there was any truth to what Carolyn said about her husband. I didn't think I could go off and hunt deer without having things settled in my mind.

I got that from my old man. Even when the black Hudson and the Stetson hats were gone, when we lived out of an old grey Plymouth and squatted like fruit pickers at the edge of a field and drew pictures in the dirt like the cowboys we saw in the movies, we were keeping things in order. The pictures we drew were about the work we were doing and how we were going to finish it.

I didn't know what to think about Carolyn or Nick Pergamino. I wanted to believe women, and I wanted to trust her, but for all I knew, she had spun a long tale about her husband so it wouldn't look as if she was just stepping out on him for her own entertainment.

I did know that if I decided to go deer hunting, I would wait around on Monday evening to see if she would call, and then, whether she did or didn't, I still wouldn't have things resolved.

Back to the more practical side, what I thought of as the Hudson side, I knew that if I left on Monday morning I would have enough time to go to Bakersfield, Merced, and Turlock and get back before the rush of Labor Day weekend. The trip would eat up most of my hundred-dollar bonus, but it would help me answer some questions. It would also keep me from sitting around waiting for the phone to ring, and it might keep me from digging myself in deeper. Not that I didn't want more, because I did—but with a little distance and clear thinking, I knew it wasn't going to last forever. To the contrary, it could end at any time, and if Nick Pergamino was as dangerous as Carolyn had suggested, the end might be more than just a friendly parting.

When I went to bed that night, I heard the locomotive rumbling where it was parked next to the train station in back of the apartment house. I realized it had been idling there since I had come home from work.

* * * * *

Broad daylight on Monday morning made my course of action seem even more reasonable. I cashed my checks as soon as the bank opened, and on my way back to my apartment I saw

201

the 1964 Buick parked in front of the building where Nick Pergamino had his insurance office.

The locomotive was still idling and my nerves were a little jangled as I dialed Carolyn's number. I hadn't called her before, so I didn't know what to expect.

Her voice was clear and cheerful as she said, "Hello."

"Carolyn," I said. "This is Tommy."

"Oh? I thought you'd be at work."

"We finished that orchard yesterday. Actually, we finished the whole season. I'm going to be gone for a couple of days, looking at some other things. I didn't know whether you'd call, and I didn't want you to worry."

"That's nice of you. I suppose you need to line up more work. Is it very far away?"

I had decided earlier not to explain any more than I needed to, and I had already slipped once because I didn't like the feeling of being dishonest, but I made myself bear down. "Usually not," I said.

"Well, be careful. I'll miss you."

"Oh, I'll miss you, too. Be sure of that."

* * * * *

I made the long, hot drive to Bakersfield with the window down and the radio turned up. I smelled the first oil rigs in the heat of the late afternoon, and I drove past trucking yards, hay lots, farm implement dealers, stacks of cotton bales, and corrals full of feed and dairy cattle. I had heard of Bakersfield as a place where there was always work and money, but none of it interested me now.

I found a motel called the Maverick, a place that had weekly rates and kitchenettes. I took a single room for one night. After a hamburger and fries with too much salt, I stopped at a bar called Guthrie's. The sun had gone down, but the air was heavy with dust and heat, so the cool atmosphere inside the bar was welcome. I had a couple of drinks and watched three fellows who looked like oilfield roughnecks shooting pool. I had thought of myself as a kind of amateur detective who was going to ask questions and get leads, but I didn't see any place to begin, so I went back to the motel.

In the morning I went to the newspaper office, where I was led into a room stacked with layers and layers of past is-sues. The sheer weight and volume almost turned me back, but I took a minute and gathered my thoughts. On the drive down I had tried to estimate when the Pergaminos had lived in Bakersfield, and I had figured five years ago at the latest. So I went to the last issue of August 1964 and started working backwards.

After a while I got an idea of where and where not to look in each edition, but even at that I did not want to go too fast. The newspapers became a blur, and within an hour I found myself getting them out of order and not remembering which ones I had looked at. I went out to the front desk, asked to borrow a pen and paper, and came back to the crowded room. Now I kept track of the dates better.

Hours passed, and my eyes became tired. I went out into the glaring daylight and found a café a couple of blocks away.

I had the lunch special, drank a cup of coffee, and went back to my drudgery.

At about 3:30 in the afternoon I found what looked like an answer. A young woman named Louise Wilkinson, age twenty-five, had been found strangled in her efficiency apartment. She had been living there for about four months and was working in a nearby bar at the time of her death. She was found stretched out on the bed with no clothes on. The killer was thought to be a man, but the police had no suspects.

My mouth was dry, and I had a numb sensation in my head. I wrote down the date of the newspaper—Monday, September 28, 1963—and took the pen and pad to the front desk. I was told to wait while they sent someone to the storeroom, which I imagined to be a much larger place with various copies of past editions going who knows how far back in time. I waited about twenty minutes until a round, pale man in light brown hair brought out a copy of the same edition I had looked at. I paid a dime and walked out into the sunlight with my copy of the Bakersfield *Californian*.

* * * * *

I rolled into Merced in the evening before the sun set. My windshield had a crust of dead bugs on it, and I was sweaty and tired. I found an older motel called the Oasis, with a tall sign held up by a column of fake slanting palm trees. It was one of those places a person might see in any of a hundred highway towns, the type of motel that Carolyn's family would have stayed in when she was growing up. My room cost me a dollar less than the one in Bakersfield. The long, orange, plastic tag attached to the key rattled as I opened the door and caught a whiff of stale air. I turned on the air conditioner and settled into a chair.

After a while I gathered the energy to go out and get something to eat. I made the mistake of ordering a fried quarter of chicken, which had a thick crust of deep-fried batter and a bit of meat inside. To get the taste out of my mouth, I drank a beer in a place called the Sportsman's. Everyone including the bartender ignored me, which wasn't all bad, but it didn't incline me to stay out late.

In the morning I found the newspaper office, which was a smaller version of the one I had visited the day before. The newspapers were slimmer as well, so I made my way through them at a better pace. At a little before noon I found a second-page story about a girl named Mary Lynn Underhill, age twenty-one, who was found dead in her room in a downtown hotel. She was discovered on her bed, unclothed, and police thought she had been strangled. She did not have any known employment, and she had been living in Merced for only a few months. The date of the article was Tuesday, August 10, 1965. For ten cents I had another newspaper for my collection.

* * * * *

Turlock was not very far from Merced, north on Highway 99, so I made it there by mid-afternoon. I asked around for the newspaper office, and I was told that the best bet for finding older news articles was the Modesto *Bee*. So I drove the rest of the way to Modesto and got a room in an old hotel downtown for six dollars. I felt I was saving both time and money, so I went out and found a small restaurant that served a dinner special of roast beef and gravy.

Partway through my meal I got to feeling guilty about these poor working girls who never got a chance. It made me think of Marcie, and I realized I hadn't thought much of her since I got caught up with Carolyn and her stories about Nick. Marcie had faded into the background as someone who might have been a victim of the possibly dangerous husband of a woman I was fooling around with, and now it seemed like a crummy way for her to be defined. Here were these dead girls, one after another, and here I was, enjoying a roast beef dinner. I got past my guilty feeling by telling myself that at least I was doing something and at least someone cared.

* * * * *

I combed through the back issues of the Modesto *Bee* as if I was an old pro, sure of what I was looking for and sure I would find it. I think I was expecting too much, though, and I ran out of gas at about 11:30 in the morning. Everything began to drift on me, and for the first time since Bakersfield I began to wonder whether I would find what I was looking for.

I went out of the newspaper office and wandered down the street. Everyone looked like strangers from a distant city, and I had to remind myself that Modesto was just a big town not more than two hundred miles from where I lived. It was a known quantity, and somewhere behind the impersonal fronts of these buildings there was information to be known. I just had to buck myself up.

After lunch in a dim café I went back to the newspaper office and tried another approach. I read the name plate on the first desk beyond the counter and spoke to the girl sitting there.

"Are you Julie?"

"Yes, I am. Can I help you?"

She was about twenty years old, with platinum hair and a bright smile. I didn't feel stupid talking to her.

"Maybe so," I said. "I was looking through your old papers, and I got bogged down."

"What were you looking for?"

"A news article. I heard about a girl, or a young woman, who was found dead a few years ago in Turlock, but I couldn't find anything about it. I went through a stack of papers, but I didn't feel I was getting anywhere. Actually, I know I wasn't."

She drew her brows together. "How long ago did it happen?"

"I'm not sure. I think it might have been from about 1966 to 1968."

"Maybe one of the reporters would know. Let me go ask."

She turned and walked away, not a bad distraction in itself, and disappeared through a doorway into a large room in back.

She came out several minutes later with a middle-aged, gaunt-looking man. He had straight, dark brown hair, shadows under his eyes, and blue veins sticking out on the pale undersides of his forearms. He looked to me as if he could have been a murder suspect himself.

"This is Les," she said. "He's been a reporter here for quite a while."

"Thanks." I smiled to her and then met the eyes of the reporter. "I know this is kind of vague," I said, "but I'm trying to find information about a woman in Turlock about two or three years ago. She would have been a young woman, maybe a barmaid or cocktail waitress."

"Dead?"

"Yes, but I don't know the details."

"It sounds familiar. I don't remember her name, but I think it was June or July of '67. Let me go see." He pointed at a chair by the window. "Have a seat."

I did as he told me. The chair was straight-backed, about a hundred years old and creaky, and not much for comfort. From where I sat, the counter blocked my view of Julie and any of the others at their desks.

Les reappeared about ten minutes later and tossed me a glance. I stood up and moved to the counter.

"I found something that might be what you're looking for. First weekend in July, 1967. Young woman, twenty-three years old. I did the story. It was no good."

I frowned. "The story?"

"What the guy did."

"Oh. Can I get the article?"

His eyes went over me. "You didn't know her, did you?"

I shook my head. "No, but something similar happened to a girl I did know."

"None of my business, but I hope they hang the son of a bitch if they ever catch him." His Adam's apple bobbed. "Julie can get you a copy of that edition."

A few minutes later, Julie handed me a newspaper that had the date of Monday, July 3, 1967. I thought I had already gone through that date, but the paper itself did not look familiar. I gave Julie ten cents and turned the pages until I found the story. Beverly Lane, age twenty-three and originally from Atwater, had been found in her flat in an older house in Turlock. In the words of the article, she was "spread-eagled" on her bed. Up until a week before, she had been working as a car hop in a drive-in, and then she went to work in a bar called the Hideaway. Police had no suspects, though the nature of the crime led them to believe the killer was a male.

I felt as if I had the wind knocked out of me once again. It was all too real and familiar. As I stared at the article—the same story with a different name and age–I realized I had no further business in the newspaper office and I was done with Modesto and Turlock as well. I walked out into the bright daylight and found my way to my car. It was hot to the touch and like an oven inside. I rolled down the window and got out onto the highway, where I stepped on the gas and let things roll.

Ever since Bakersfield I had gone through little towns and big ones. Anyone could remember the bigger towns like Fresno, Madera, Merced, and Modesto, but on this day I made

myself remember the names of some of the smaller ones—
Delano, Fowler, Berenda, Delhi, Ceres, Ripon. I had driven
that whole length a few times before, and from one trip to the
next, these were the little places I wouldn't remember until I
drove past them again. Today they seemed like Louise Wilkinson, Mary Lynn Underhill, and Beverly Lane—girls who
had become names and ages and dates of death in old newspapers stacked in back rooms. Not one of them had rated a
photograph.

Neither had Marcie, now that I thought of it. Marcie Paulson. Her family and friends would remember her, but if some
stranger happened to be reading the newspaper a few years
from now, she would be just another girl who came to a bad
end.

* * * * *

Back at my apartment, everything was still and quiet. I put
the three newspapers in my gun closet, an old homemade
thing I had bought second-hand. It looked more like a storage
cabinet than anything else, as it was made of dull-stained plywood with no glass. It had a simple cabinet lock and a small
porcelain knob that might have come off a screen door from
an earlier era.

I sat in my armchair and went to work on a six-pack of
Coors in the can. From time to time my gaze settled on the
cabinet where I had my information safe under lock and key,
and once in a while my eyes would rest on the black Hudson
in the picture frame. Then I would go back to brooding about

Nick Pergamino, everybody's friend in the dim light of a bar-room, and a prowler of the night after that. I wondered if he found anyone to go skiing with on Labor Day weekend.

From there I would return to the question from earlier in the week, of how I was going to spend the next few days. By the time I finished my six-pack, I decided I was going to go deer hunting.

* * * * *

The next day being Friday as well as a day off, I tried to keep myself from getting into a hurry as I got my camping gear together. I had my sleeping bag, mattress, and clothes bag in a pile in the living room and was counting my rifle shells when the phone rang.

It was Carolyn, and her voice sounded nervous. "Tommy, I've been worried about you. Where have you been?"

"Oh, I've been out like I told you."

"What are you doing right now?"

"I'm getting ready to go hunting." I glanced at the rifle shells I had set on the table.

"What's that noise?"

"It's the train. They left an engine here sometime during the night."

"So you're going to go hunting. When?"

"In a little while. I'm getting my stuff together now."

"Oh. Would it be all right if I came over?"

I felt things knot up. "Well, um, do you think it would be a good time? I mean, is the coast clear?"

"Sure. It's all right."

"Okay. I'll leave the door open."

I cracked the front door a couple of inches and went back to what I was doing. I put my rifle shells, knife, pocket watch, and hunting license in a kit bag and laid it on top of the duffel bag. Then I slipped my deer rifle into the case, zipped it shut, and laid it across the sleeping bag and mattress. Back at the gun closet, I looked at my brother's .357 for a long moment before I shook my head and locked the cabinet.

I had my back to the entryway when I heard Carolyn's light knock. I turned as the door pushed open, and my tingle of excitement vanished when I saw her husband crowd in behind her and close the door.

"I'm sorry," she said. Her eyes were full of apology.

Nick made a jabbing motion, and she stepped forward. He moved aside far enough for me to see that he had a gun in his hand. It was a flat, square thing like I had seen on cops and in the movies.

"Tell him," he said.

She looked down and said, "He found out."

My mouth had gone dry and my heart was pounding, but my mind was clear. "What do you want?" I asked him.

His voice rose. "What do I want? Don't be a dummy. It's what I don't want, and it's too late for that now."

I tried to moisten my mouth as the train engine went chug-chug-chug in the background.

"Are you scared?" he said.

"Not so much."

"You should be."

"For such a small thing?"

"Small? She's got a big mouth when you know how to make her talk."

I shifted my eyes to Carolyn, and she had a helpless expression.

"He made me," she said. "He put the gun under my chin and made me tell him everything."

I turned back to him. I felt that I needed to keep him talking. I said, "I'm sorry, Nick. Once is bad enough, and three times is worse. I know it was wrong, and I apologize. But it's nothing to shoot someone over."

"Oh, you snivelin' son of a bitch." He pointed the gun at me. "It's not only enough, but it's justified. I can shoot you both deader'n a mackerel, and I'll walk free. All I need is one witness that the two of you were carryin' on, and I've already got that."

I didn't know if he was bluffing, but I tried to keep it at a low level. "Still," I said, "it's not much of a reason to have the blood of two people on your hands. And you don't know that you'll get away with it."

"Reasons. I need reasons."

Carolyn spoke. "I told him the rest, Tommy."

"The rest?"

"About the girls in the other towns." She looked good and scared now.

I brought my eyes back around to him. "So you want to keep us quiet about that?"

"What do you think?"

My mind raced for a second, and I said, in a matter-of-fact tone, "Louise Wilkinson."

His eyes narrowed, and he held the gun right on me. "Where'd you get that?"

"Not from Carolyn. I got it on my own."

"Who from?" He was taking a deep breath and stretching his upper lip over his teeth.

I took a second to observe him. He was dressed as if he had come from the office, with a white shirt and tie and his hair combed back, but he had a clouded expression and his eyes were narrow and tight.

"From a public source," I said. "Where do you think I've been the last few days?"

"I could blow a hole right through your liver."

"You ought to find out first where I have that information and whether anyone else knows where I have it."

He gave Carolyn a sidelong glance, and she shook her head.

"I don't remember any names," she said.

"Mary Lynn Underhill," I went on. "And Beverly Lane."

His hand with the gun was wavering, and he saw me looking at it. He shook the gun and held it still.

"Newspapers," I said. "Black and white and read all over."

"Where are they?"

"I'll trade you for them."

"Where are they? By God, I'll kill you if you don't tell me."

"You kill me, and you'll be a long time findin' 'em. The cops'll get here first, and they'll find 'em. They'll put two and two together, and nobody walks away."

His face was hard and tense. "You talk too much."

I shrugged. All this time, the key was in the lock of the gun cabinet, and I was afraid he was going to go there and unlock it. I looked down at my gun case to keep from looking anywhere else.

His eyes followed mine. "Goin' huntin', uh?"

"I was planning to."

"Maybe we should all go."

"Sure," I said. "We can burn the newspapers in the campfire."

He narrowed his eyes on me again. "Where are they?"

"I'll trade you."

"Quit talkin' shit."

"You let Carolyn walk outside, and I'll give them to you."

"Give 'em to me first, and she and I'll both leave."

"After you shoot me?"

He smiled. "I can shoot you first and take my chances on findin' 'em in time. You've got more to lose than I do."

I heard the train engine chugging, and I didn't think the sound would drown out a pistol shot. I licked my lips and tried to moisten my mouth again, and I was glad to see him notice it.

"Okay," I said.

I turned my back on him and walked toward the plywood cabinet. My hand was shaky as I laid my fingers on the key, and I knew I was going to have to do things just right.

John D. Nesbitt

I opened the door about three-quarters of the way and reached in to my left. The .357 was on an upper shelf, and the newspapers were in the middle. I tried my best to do everything in one smooth motion. I grabbed the papers with my left hand, tilted them up, and got my right hand on the pistol. As I stepped back and turned, I held the papers forward at a slant so they covered the gun.

"Set 'em over there," he said.

I let them slide off one another onto the floor, and his eyes followed them. Then they went wide as he saw the .357 pointed at him. His hand jerked as he pulled the trigger on the automatic. The blast filled the room, and the bullet crashed through the cabinet behind me on my left. In that instant I drew back the hammer and fired. The .357 slug caught him on the side, above the hip, and spun him halfway around as he fell to the floor. The automatic skidded under the kitchen table.

He was bleeding on the linoleum. I held my gun on him as I picked up the newspapers and set them on the coffee table. Carolyn was backed up in the corner by the door.

"Maybe you should open the door and wait outside," I said. "There's nothing to do at this point but tell the truth."

She had no sooner gone outside than I heard the sirens.

* * * * *

Several weeks later, when I was well into olive season, I received a letter with no return address. It was postmarked Tehachapi, and it had a single sheet of pink paper inside. The

216

handwriting was very neat, and I saw Carolyn's signature at the bottom. The letter said she was staying with her sister in Tehachapi and getting things straightened out. She said she was sorry I missed deer hunting with all the trouble. She went on to say that if I was ever in the neighborhood I could look her up, and she gave her sister's address. She didn't mention Nick, but she knew as well as I did that he was in jail for Marcie Paulson's murder, and if he went anywhere but San Quentin, it would be to Bakersfield, Merced, or Turlock, depending on who got their hands on him first.

After her signature she had a P.S. that said, "I hope you get a horse some day."

I smiled as I looked at the picture of the black Hudson and then put her letter back in the envelope. I thought Tehachapi was a long ways to go, and I didn't know if I would ever want to take the plunge again, but I put the envelope in my gun cabinet for safe keeping.

About the Author

John D. Nesbitt lives in the plains country of Wyoming, where he teaches English and Spanish at Eastern Wyoming College. His articles, reviews, fiction, and poetry have appeared in numerous magazines and anthologies. He has had more than thirty books published, including short story collections, contemporary novels, and traditional westerns, as well as textbooks for his courses. John has won many awards for his work, including two awards from the Wyoming State Historical Society (for fiction), two awards from Wyoming Writers for encouragement of other writers and service to the organization, two Wyoming Arts Council literary fellowships (one for fiction, one for non-fiction), a Will Rogers Medallion Award for *Dark Prairie* (a frontier mystery) and another for *Thorns on the Rose* (a poetry collection), a Western Writers of America Spur finalist award for his novel *Raven Springs*, and the Spur award itself for his short story "At the End of the Orchard" and for his novels *Trouble at the Redstone* and *Stranger in Thunder Basin*. His recent work includes *Poacher's Moon,* a contemporary novel; *Blue Horse Mesa*, a collection of western stories; and *Field Work*, a retro-noir fiction collection. Visit his website at www.johndnesbitt.com

A COLLECTION OF WESTERN STORIES

John D. Nesbitt

BLUE HORSE

M E S A

"NESBITT IS A TRUE ARTIST."
—WESTERN AMERICAN LITERATURE

Published by SpeakingVolumes

Visit us at www.speakingvolumes.us

John D. Nesbitt

BLACK HAT BUTTE

BUTTE

"NESBITT IS A TRUE ARTIST."
—WESTERN AMERICAN LITERATURE

Published by Speaking Volumes

Visit us at www.speakingvolumes.us

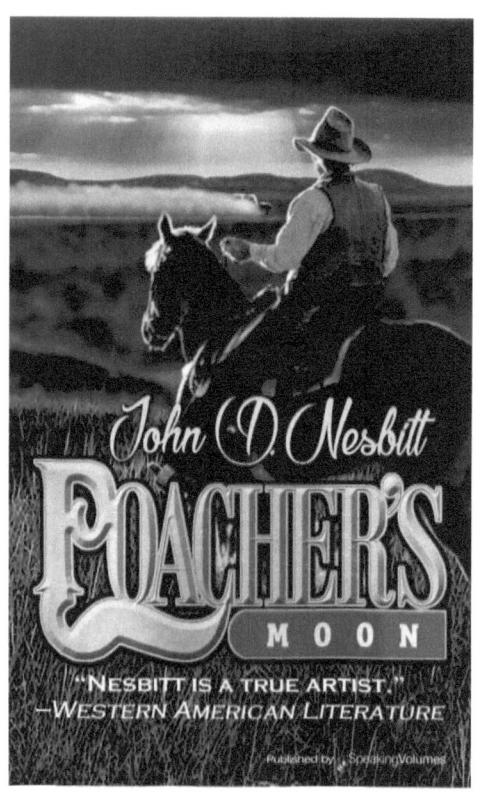

Visit us at www.speakingvolumes.us

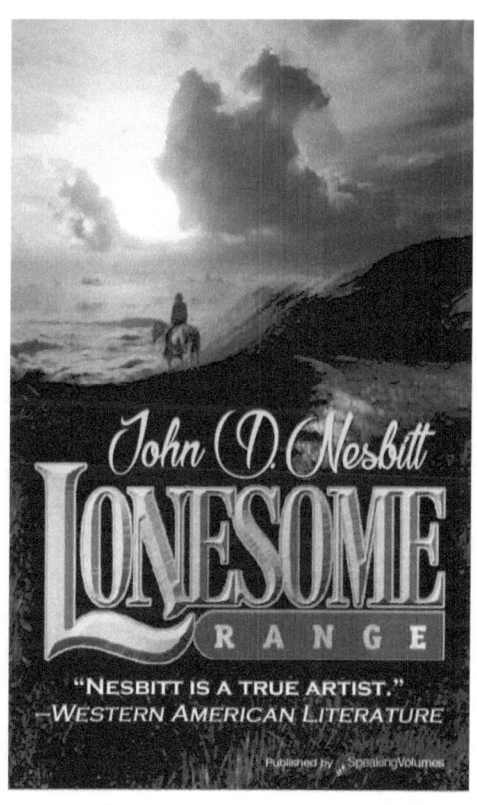

"NESBITT IS A TRUE ARTIST."
—WESTERN AMERICAN LITERATURE

Visit us at www.speakingvolumes.us

Visit us at www.speakingvolumes.us

Sign up for free and bargain books

Join the Speaking Volumes mailing list

Text

ILOVEBOOKS

to 22828 to get started.

Message and data rates may apply.

FOR MORE EXCITING BOOKS, E-BOOKS, AUDIOBOOKS AND MORE

visit us at
www.speakingvolumes.us